Little People, BIG DREAMS™
STAN LEE

Written by
Maria Isabel Sánchez Vegara

Illustrated by
Ana Albero

Frances Lincoln
Children's Books

This is the amazing story of a little boy named Stanley. He lived in New York City with his family. Like many amazing stories, his began with a dream: one day, he would write a great book like the ones he loved reading.

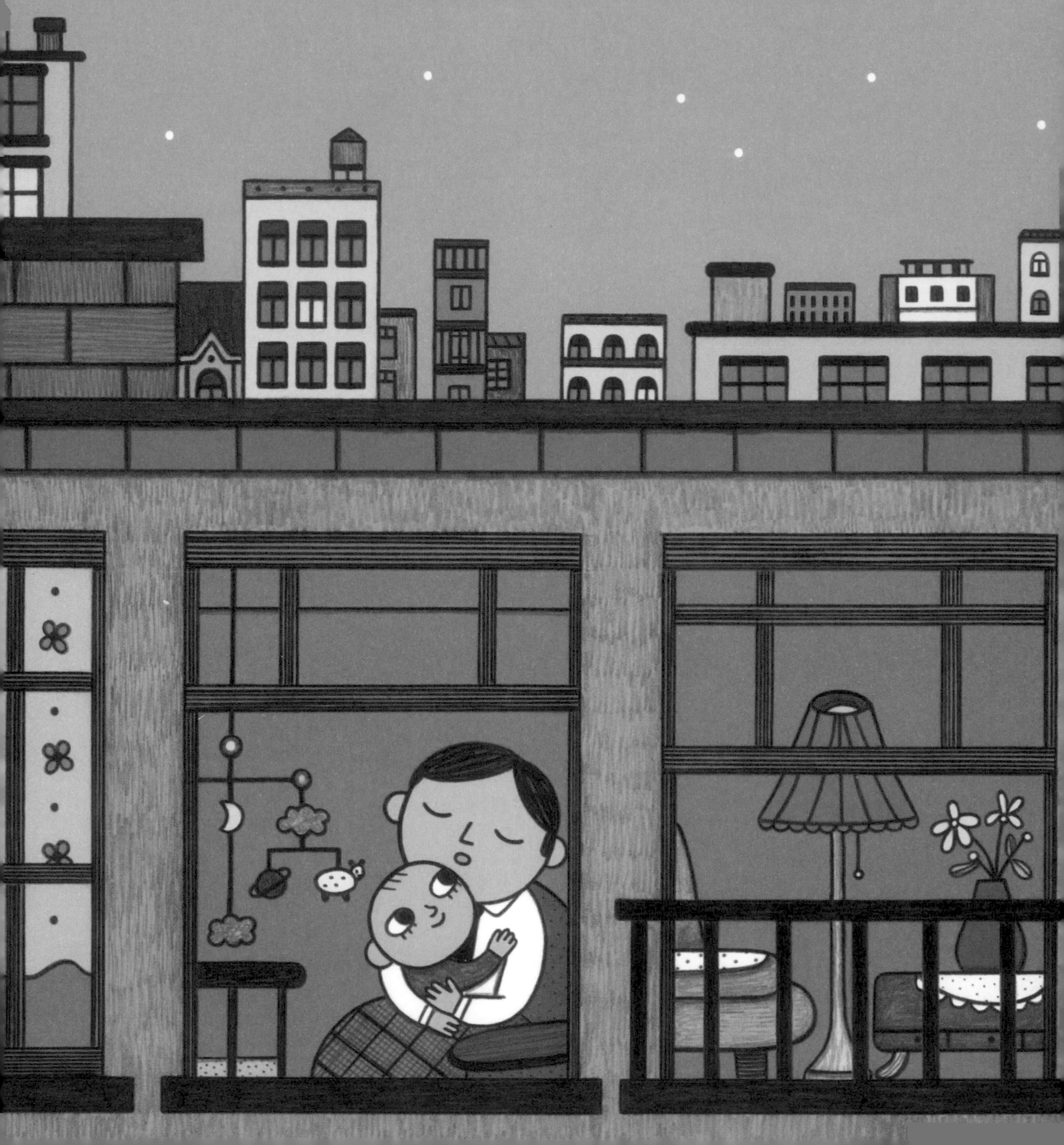

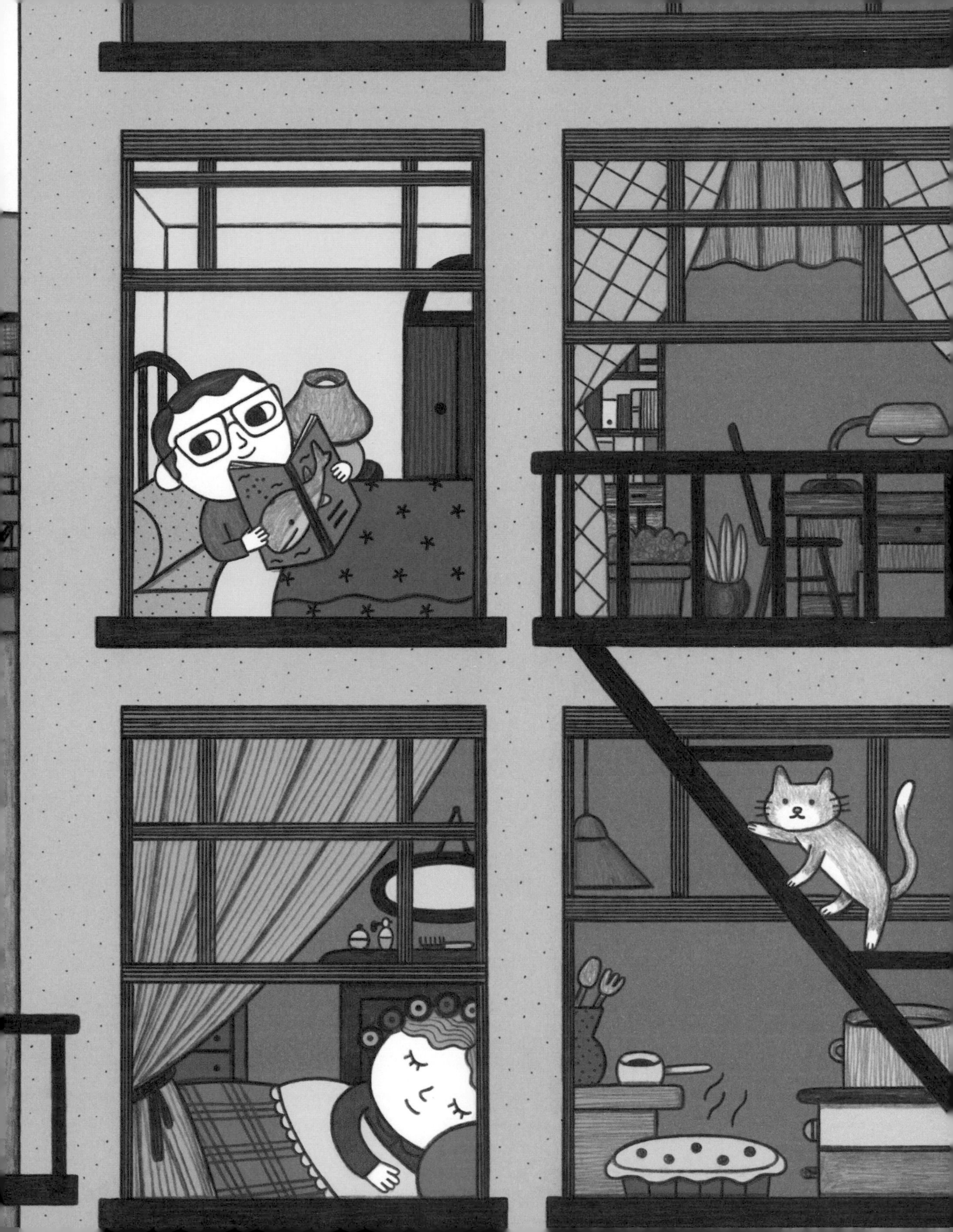

Stanley's most beloved treasure was a simple book stand. It meant he could keep reading while having dinner. He liked reading so much that if no books were around, he would entertain himself by studying the label on a ketchup bottle.

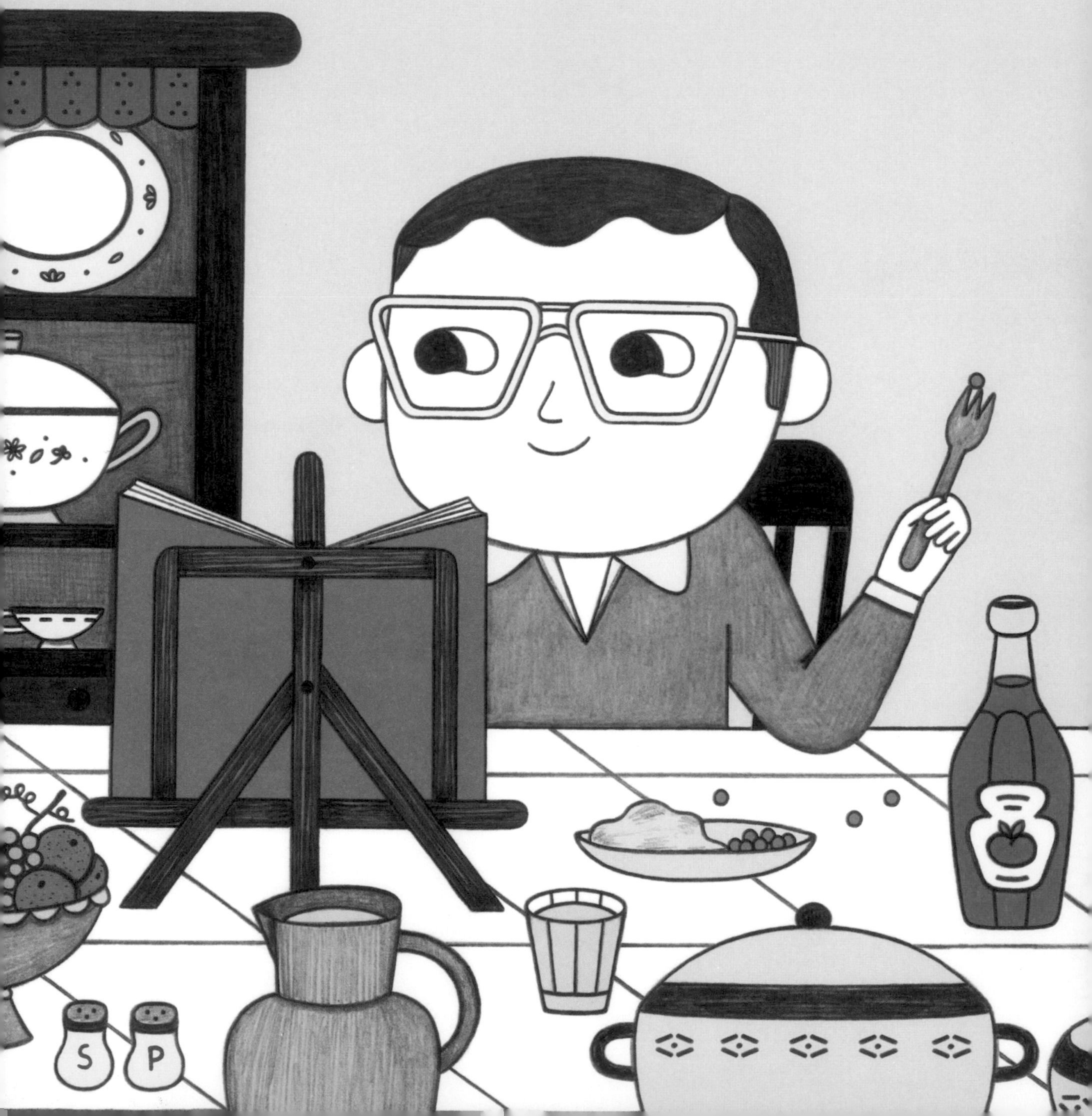
S
P

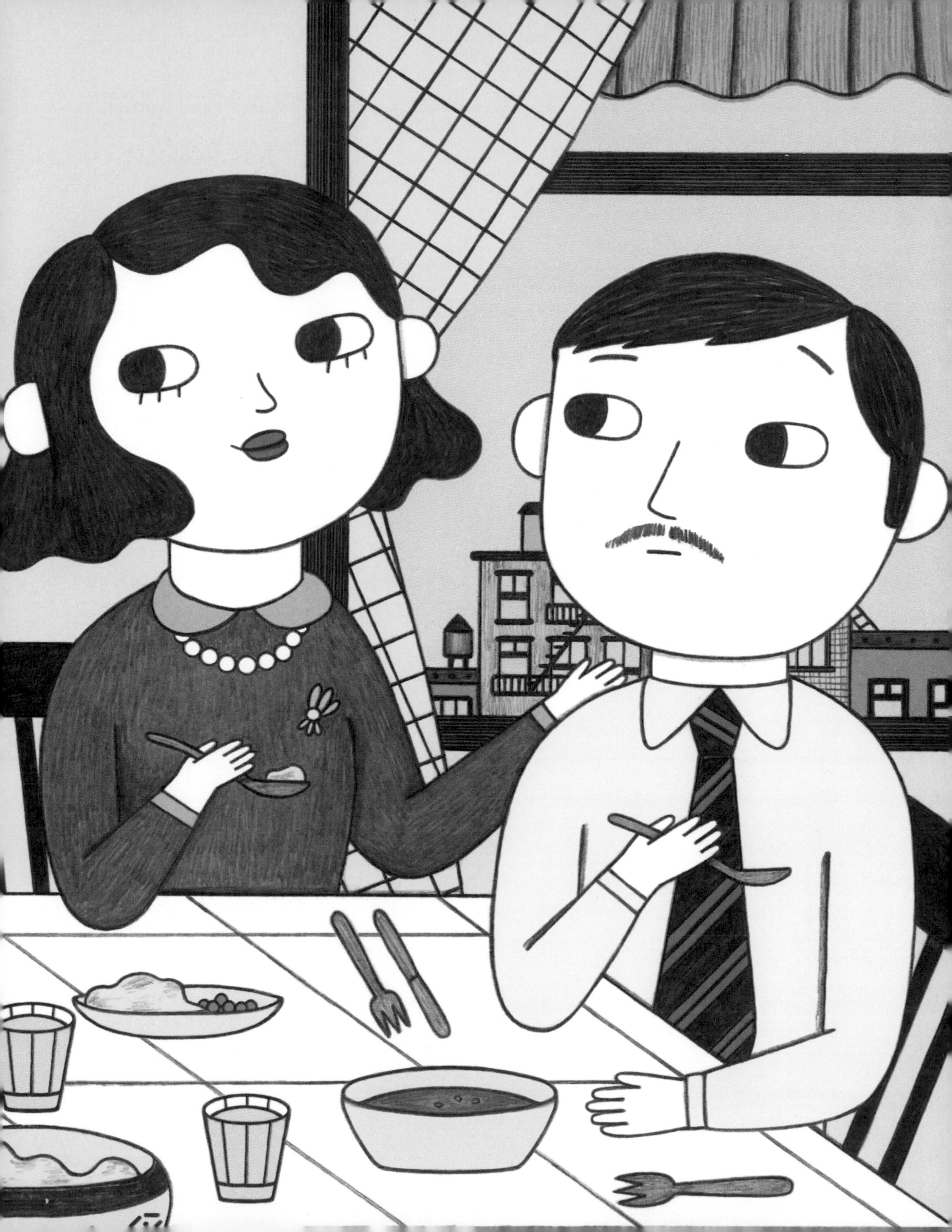

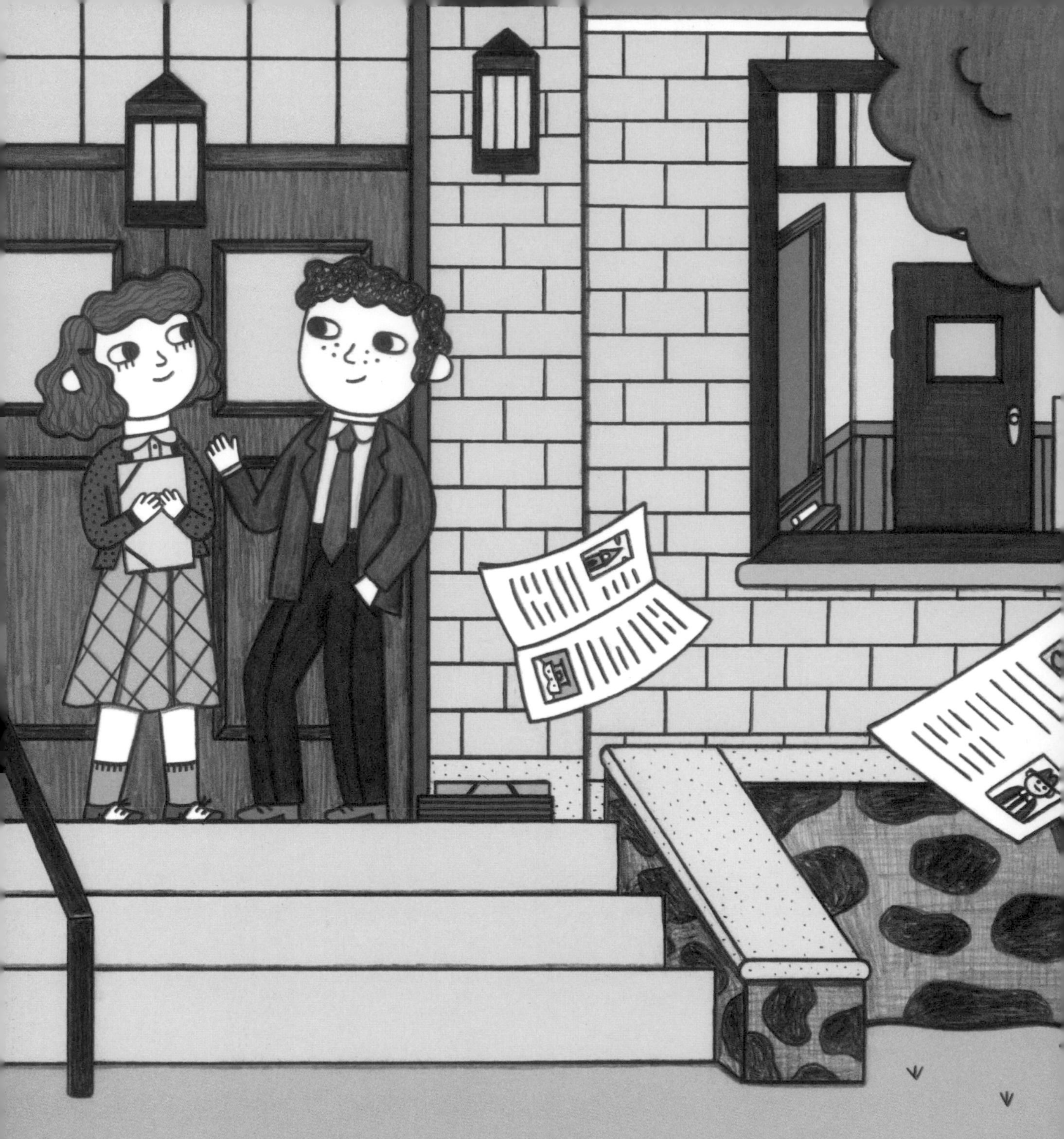

One day, he took part in a writing competition run by a local newspaper. The challenge was to find the most exciting news story of the week. When Stanley's story placed in the top ten, he felt his life as a writer had begun!

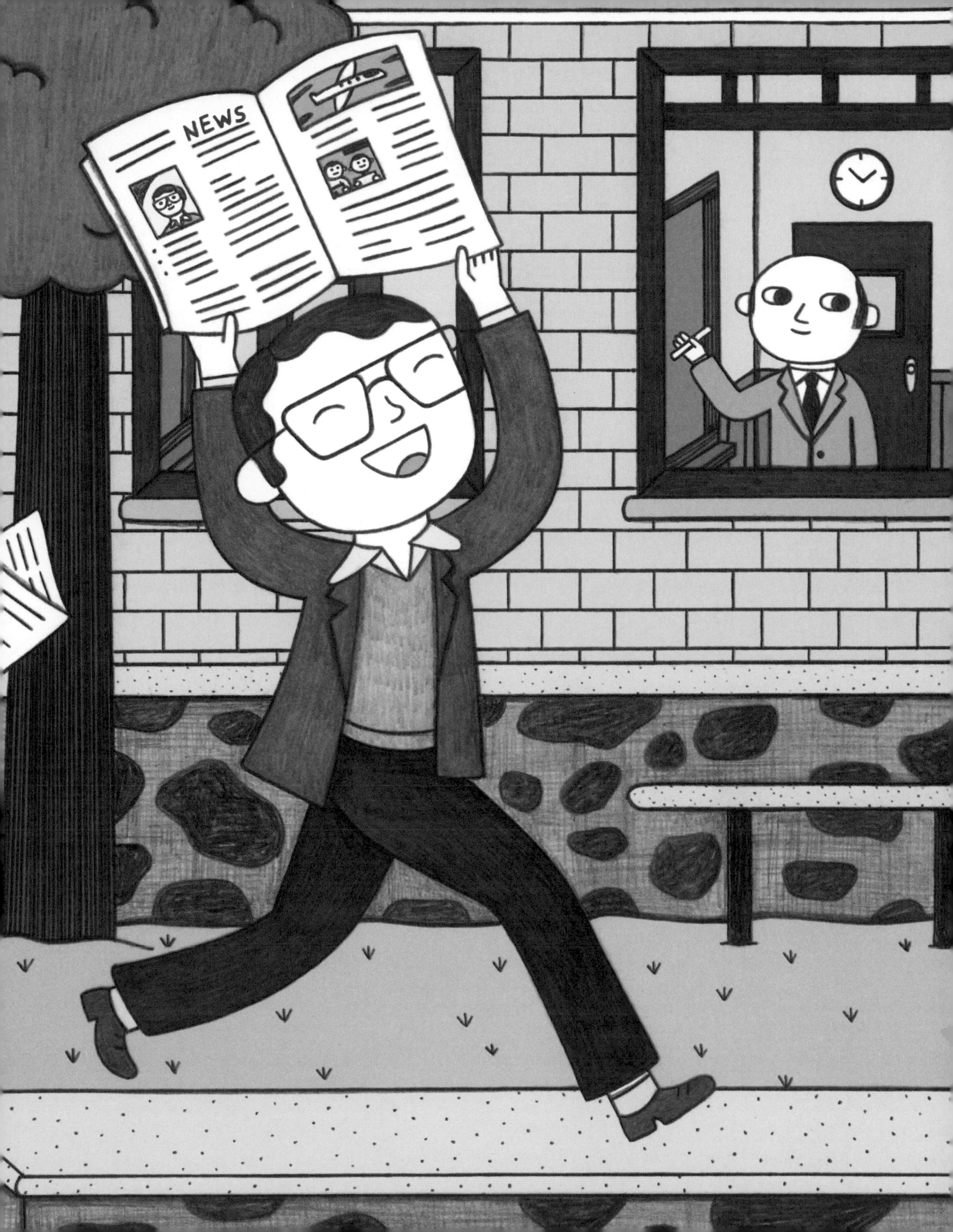
NEWS

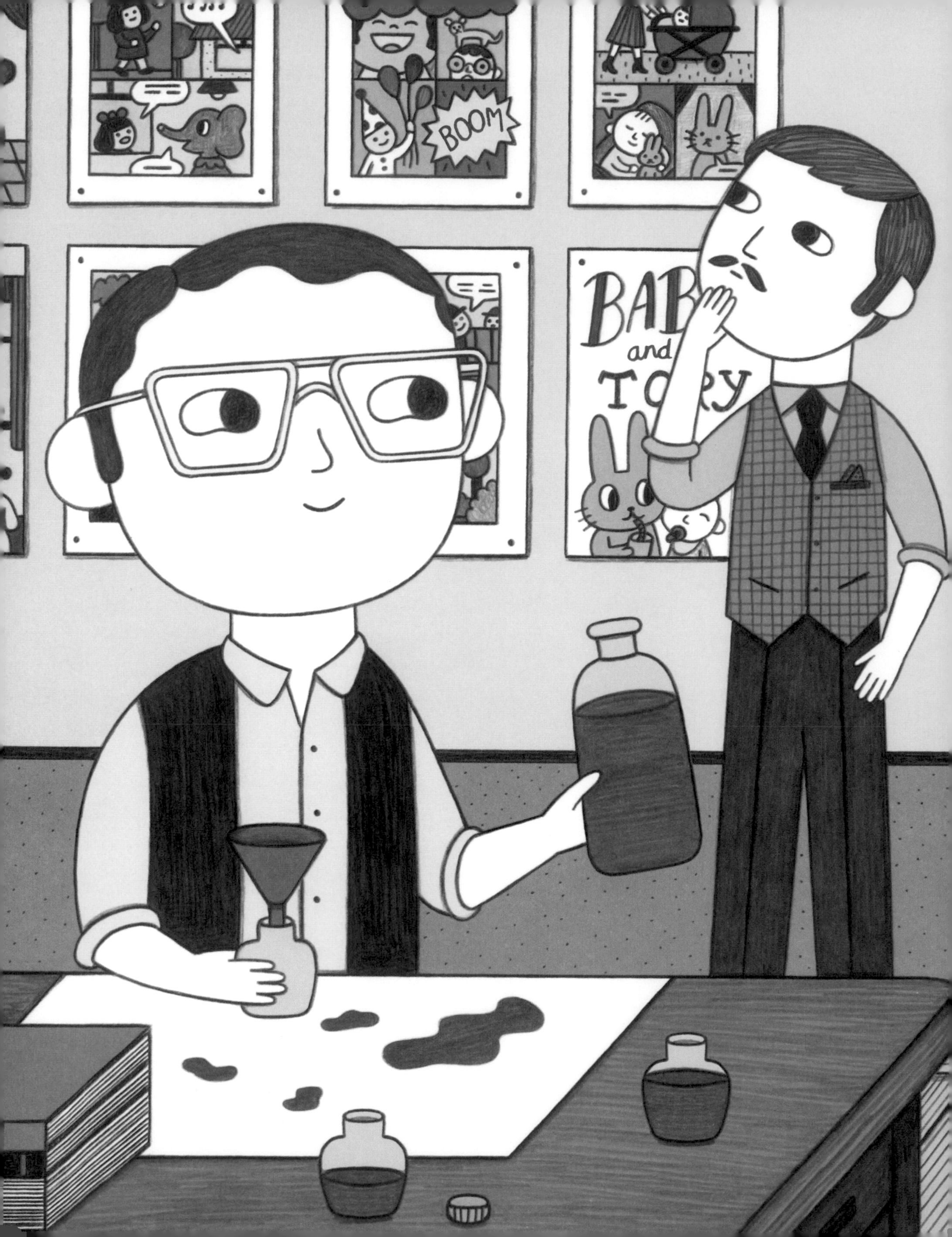
BOOM
and

After finishing high school, he got a job as an assistant at a publishing house. There, illustrators and writers joined forces to create comic books. His first duty was refilling the inkwells. Stanley thought it was the most important task in the universe.

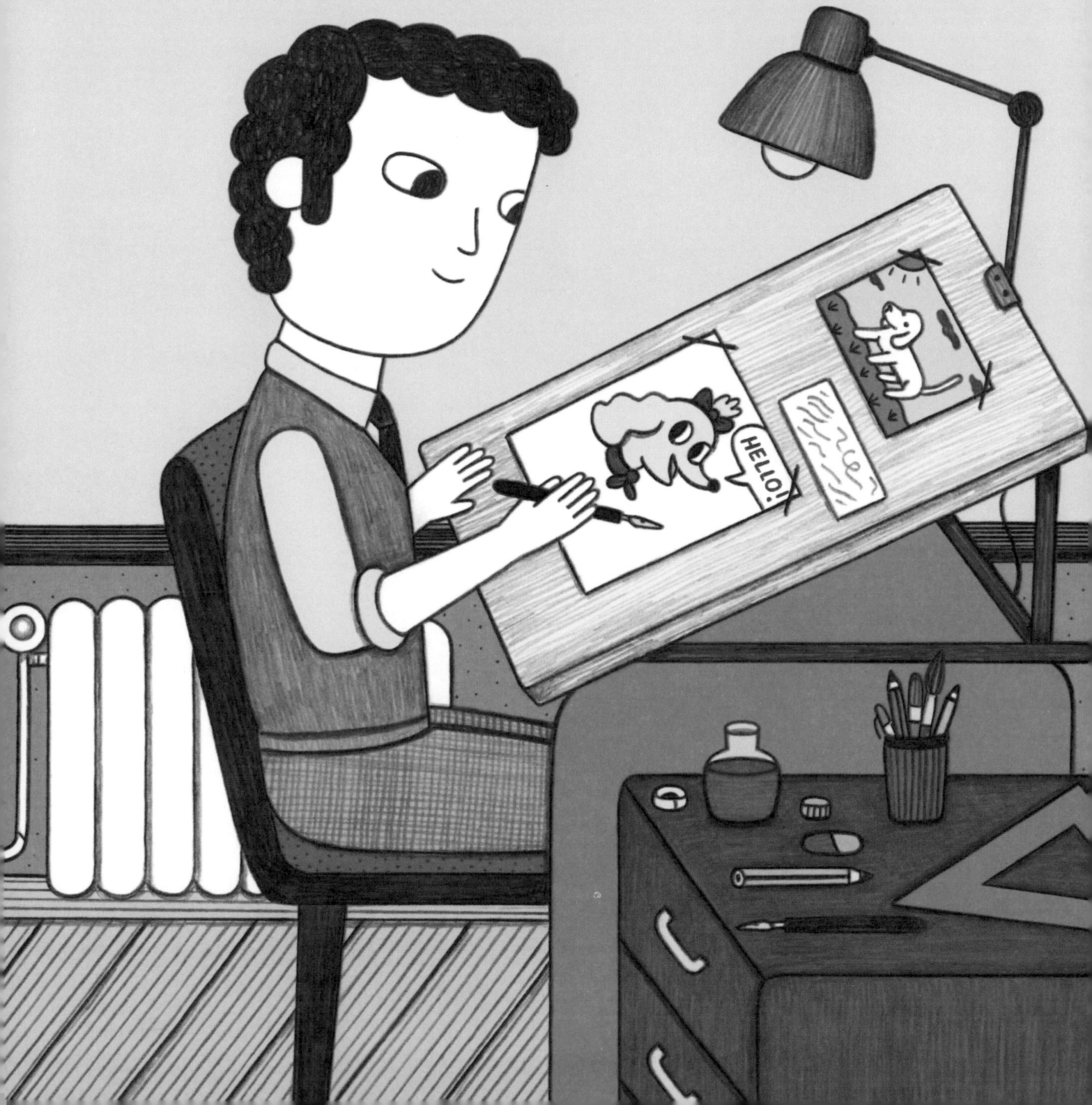
HELLO!

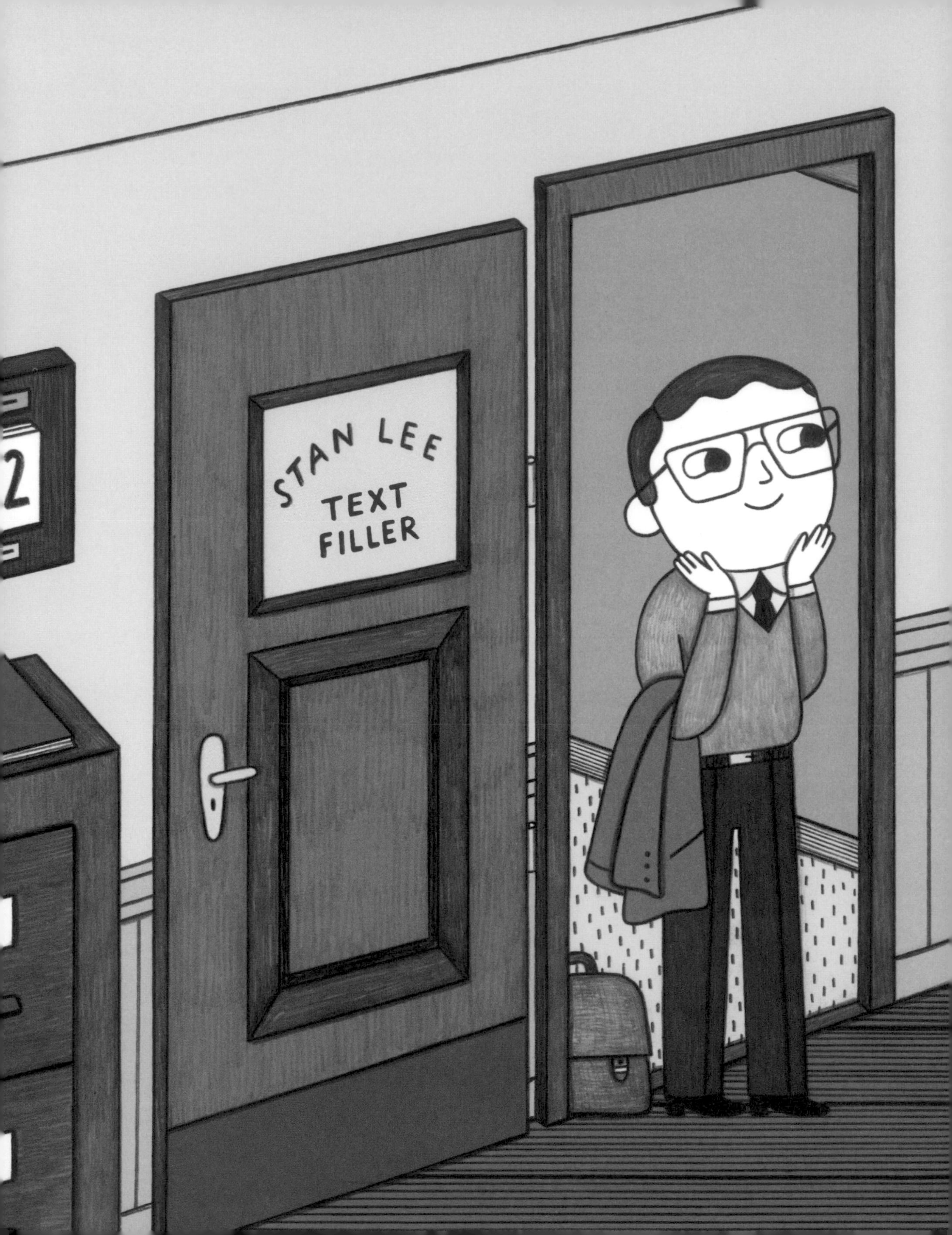
STAN LEE
TEXT
FILLER

His hard work paid off when he got the chance to write some text for a Captain America adventure. He decided to go by a pen name: Stan Lee. Little did he know that one day this name would be famous.

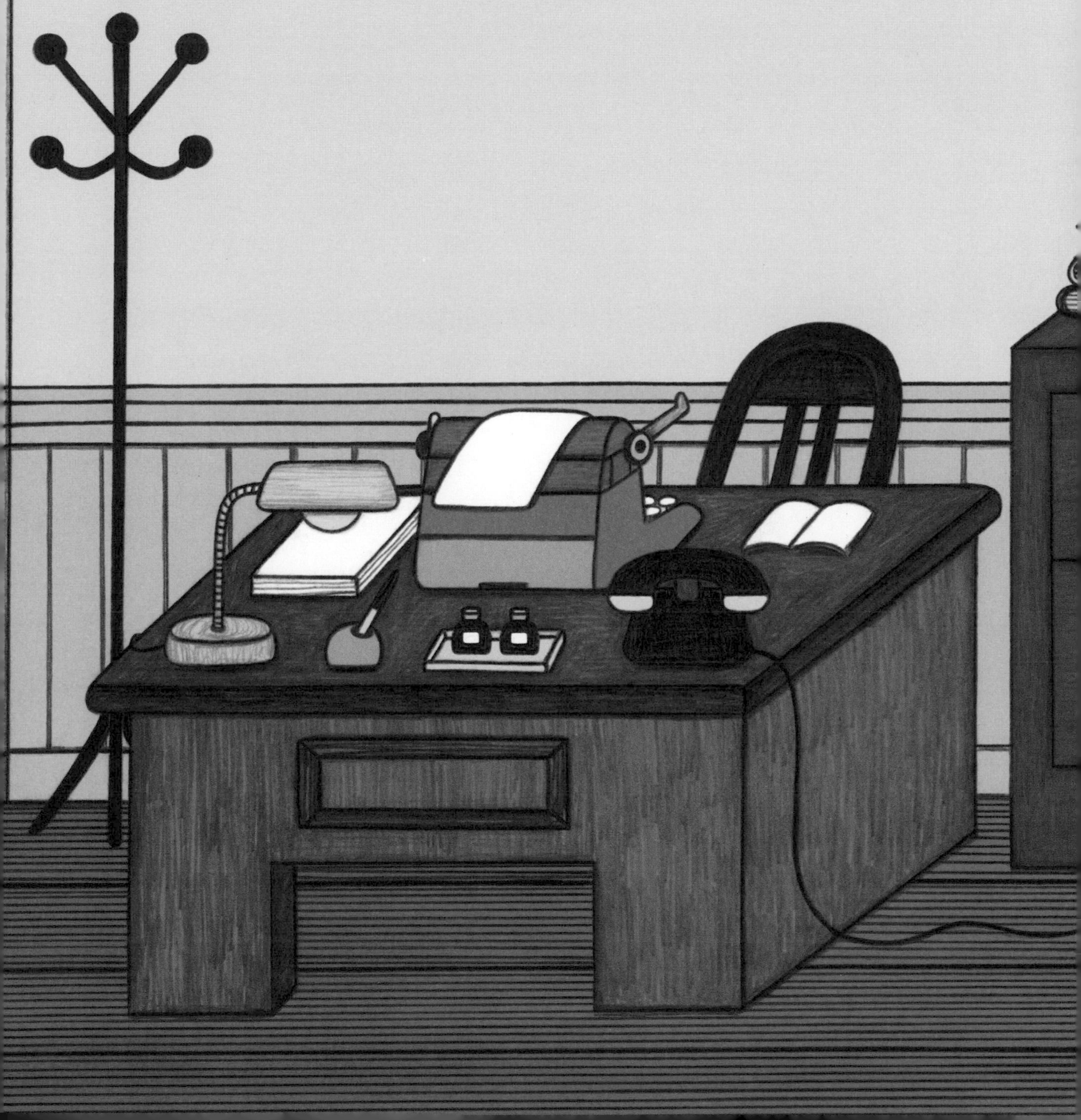

Before long, Stan was writing comics in any genre: romance, western, horror, science fiction . . .

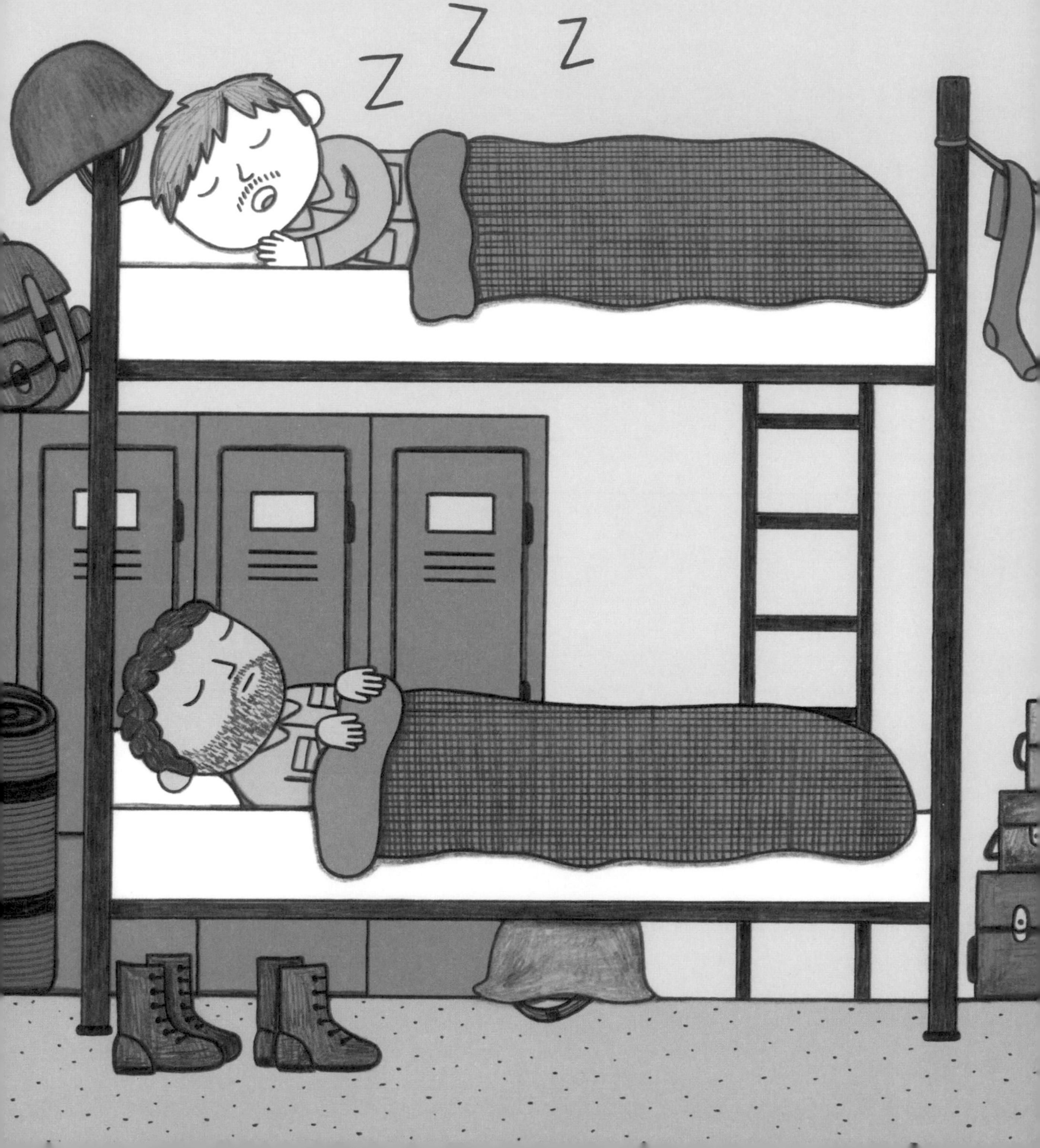
Z Z Z

Even in the army during the Second World War, he spent the weekends writing stories to send to his publisher. It was exhausting!

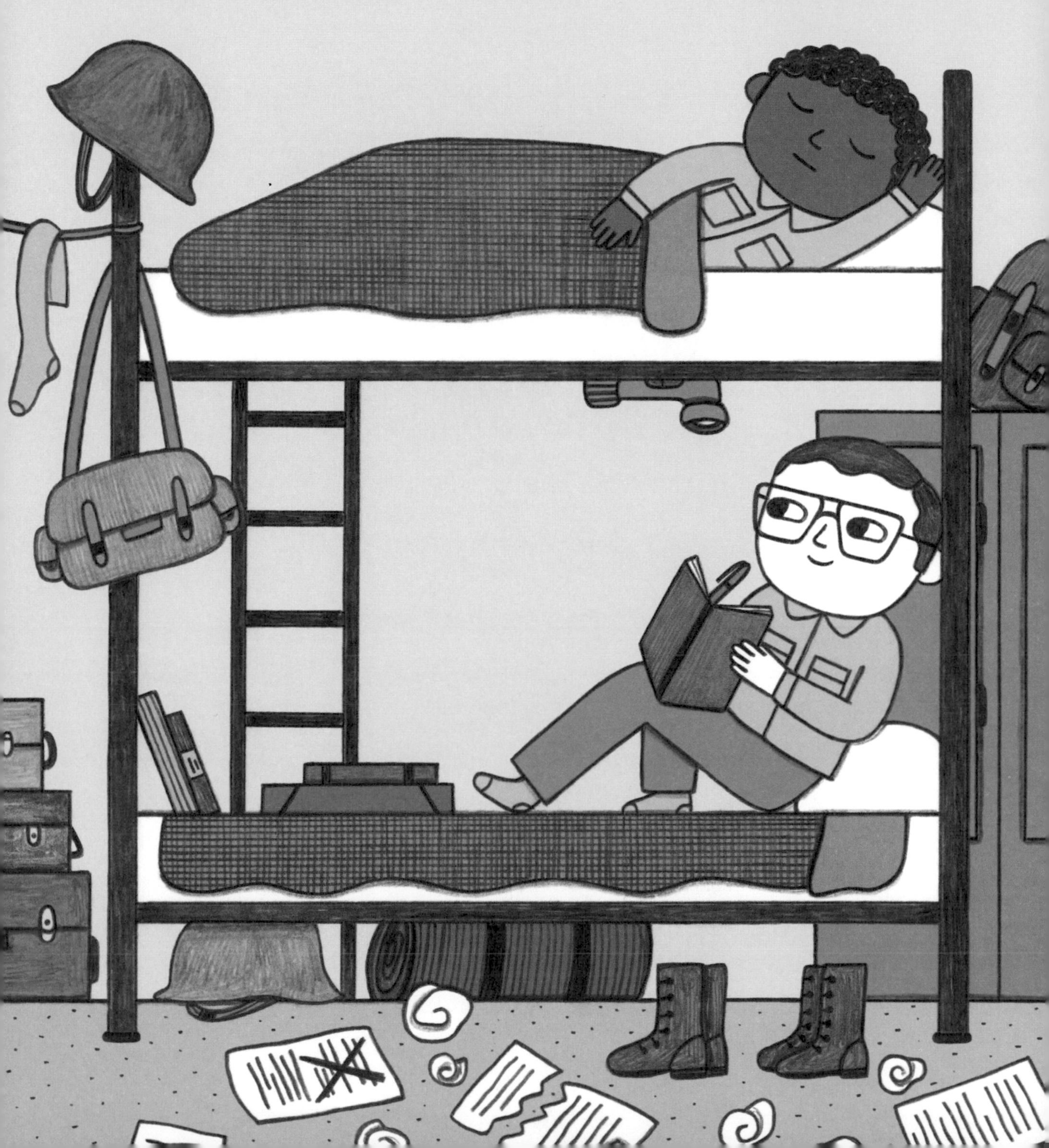

Back home, when he was asked to come up with a traditional superhero squad, Stan thought of quitting his job. He longed to write about characters who felt real. Luckily, his wife, Joan, had great advice: create superheroes as human as he was.

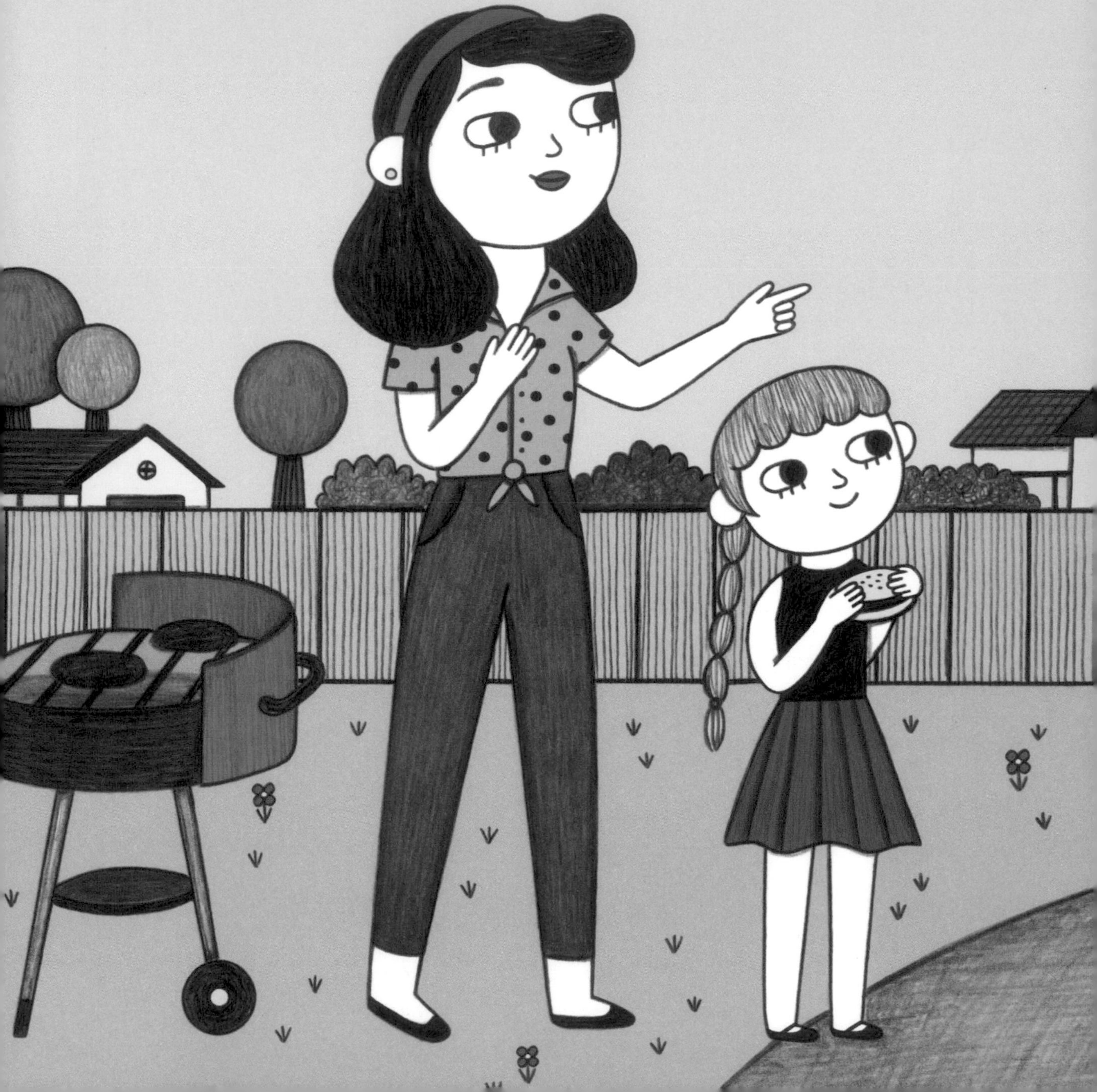

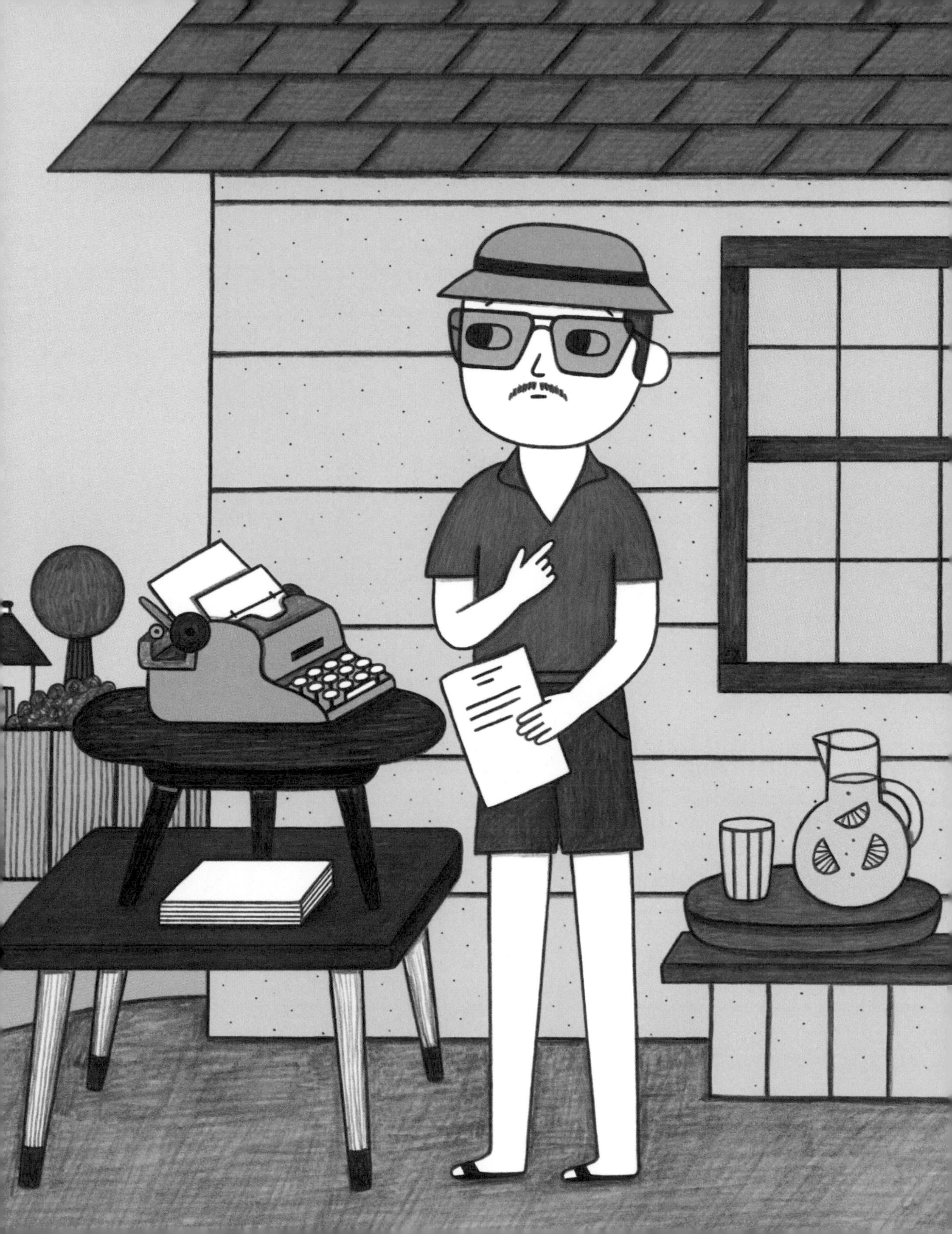

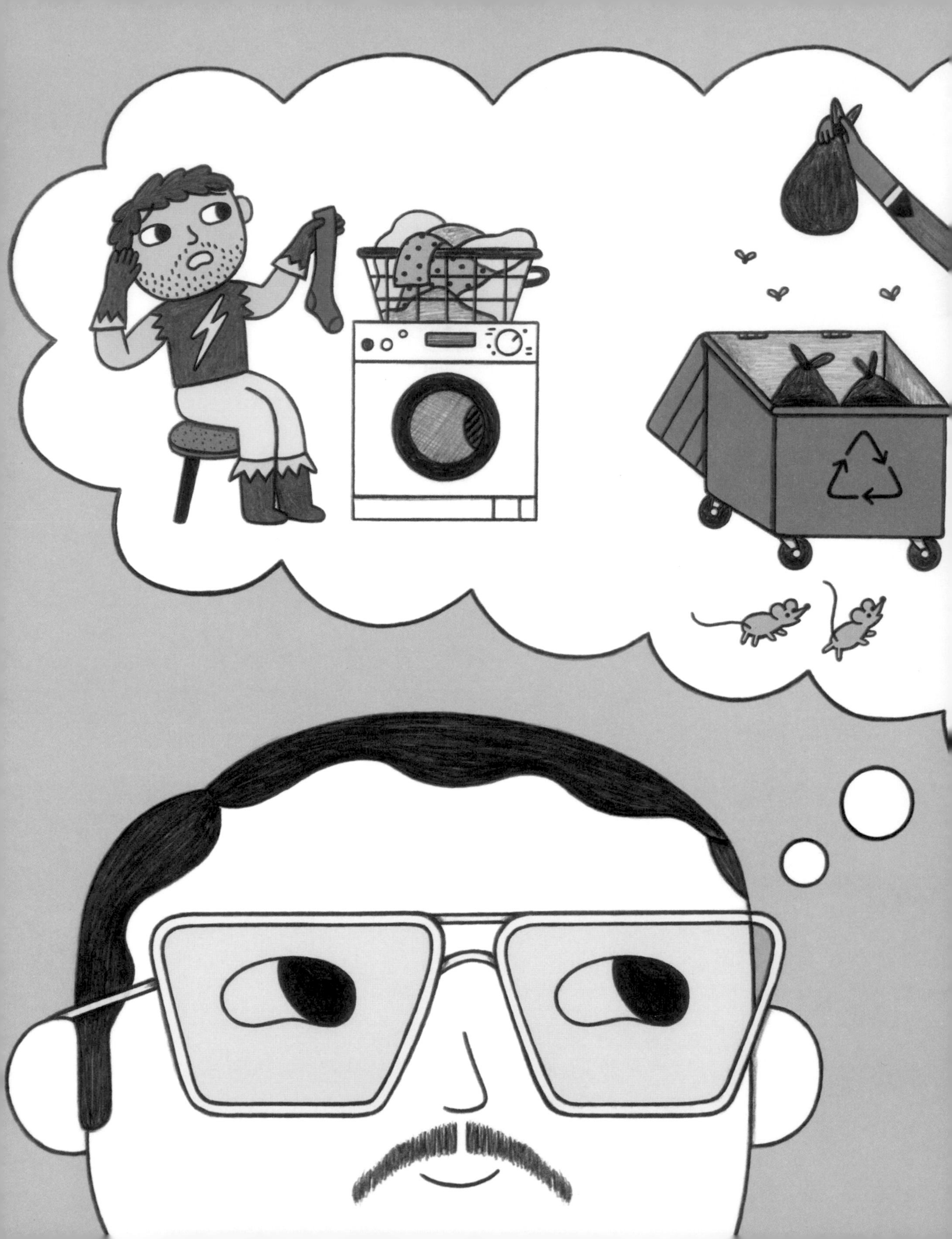

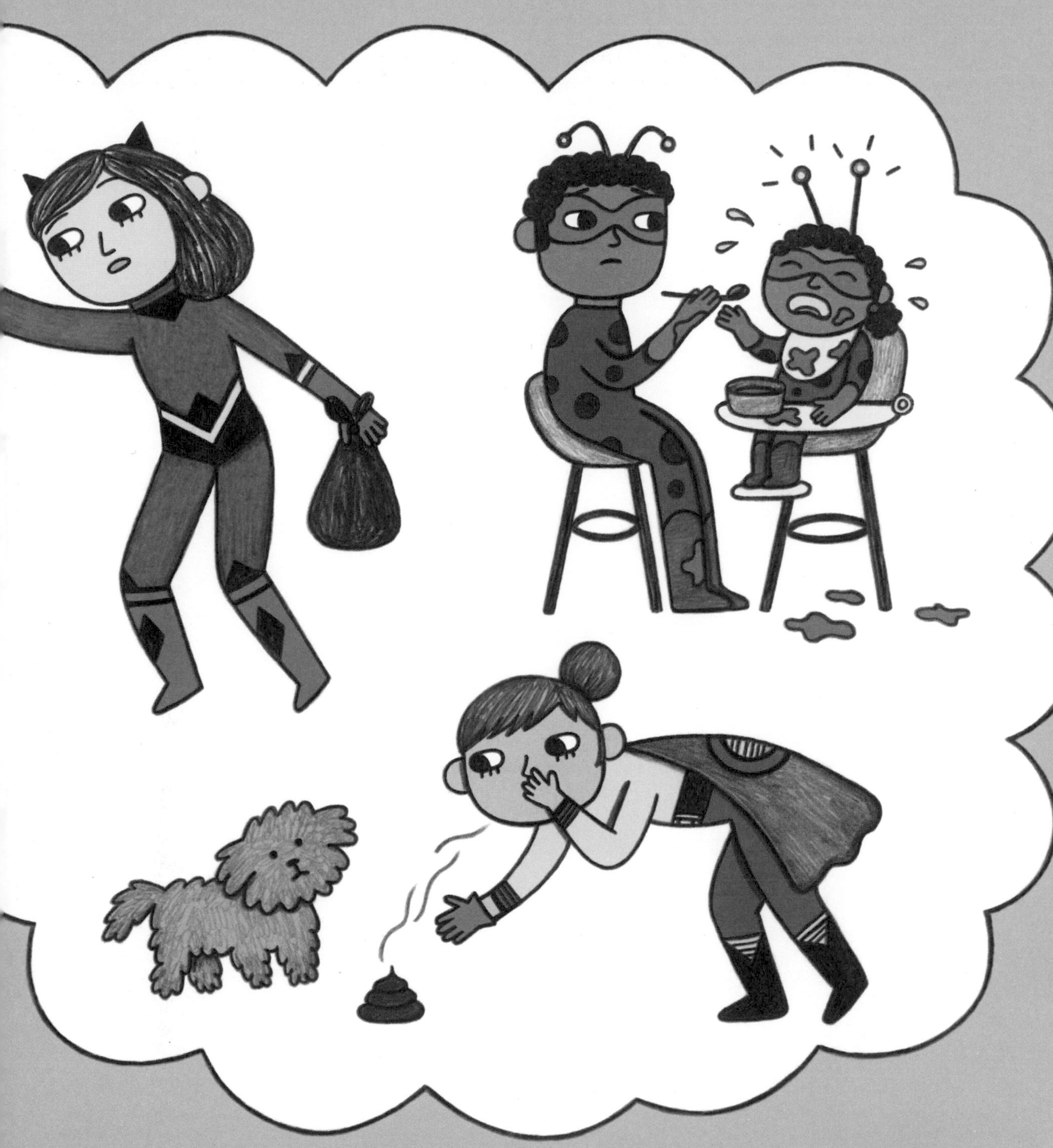

Stan listened to her wise words and made his characters imperfect. They had amazing powers but were also just like regular people. Sometimes they were bored, sad, angry, or even worried about everyday things like paying bills.

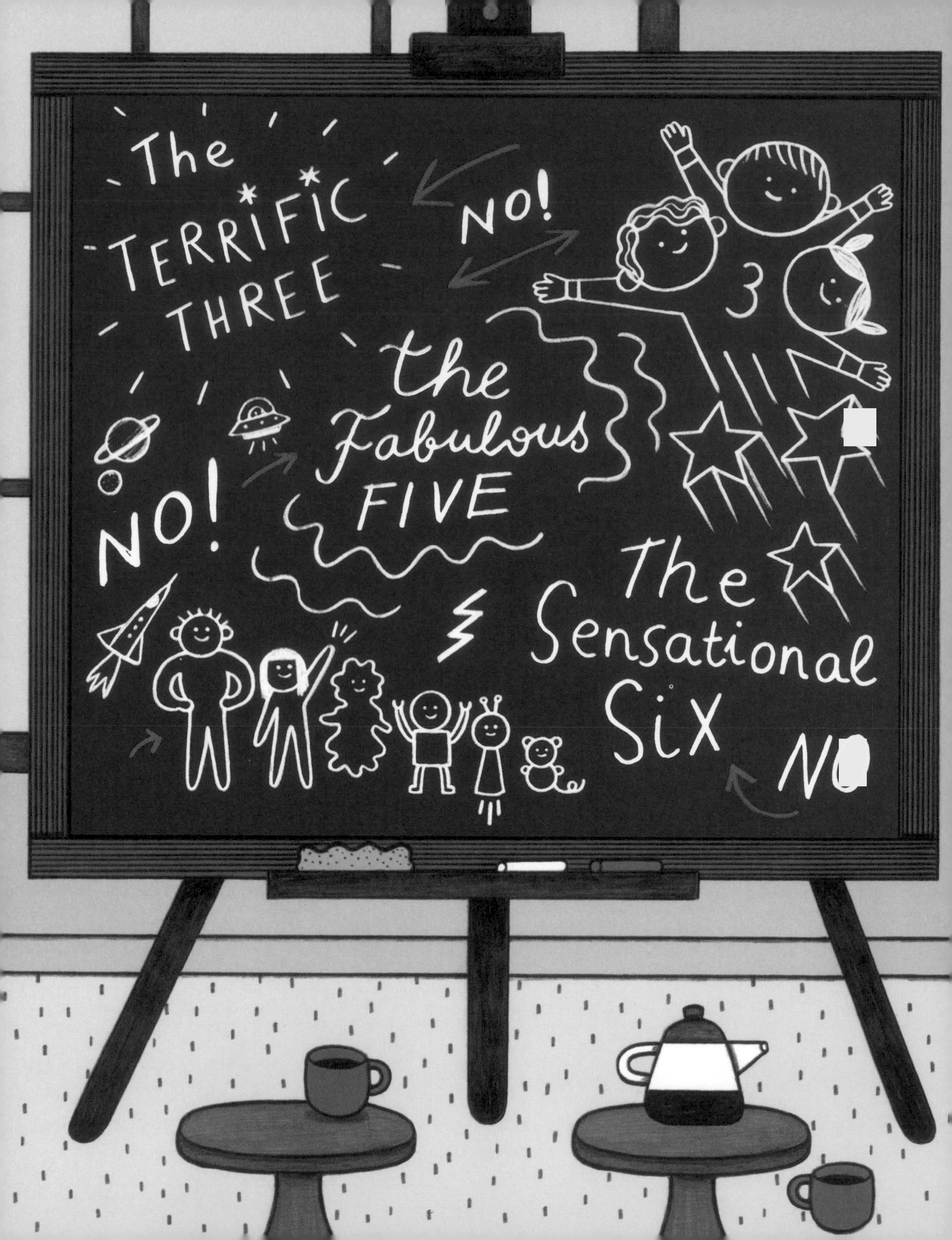
The TERRIFIC THREE
NO!
the Fabulous FIVE
NO!
The Sensational Six
N

He teamed up with an artist named Jack Kirby to create "The Fantastic Four," a group of astronauts who gained powers after a space accident. It became a hit and made his publishing company one of the coolest in the comic world.

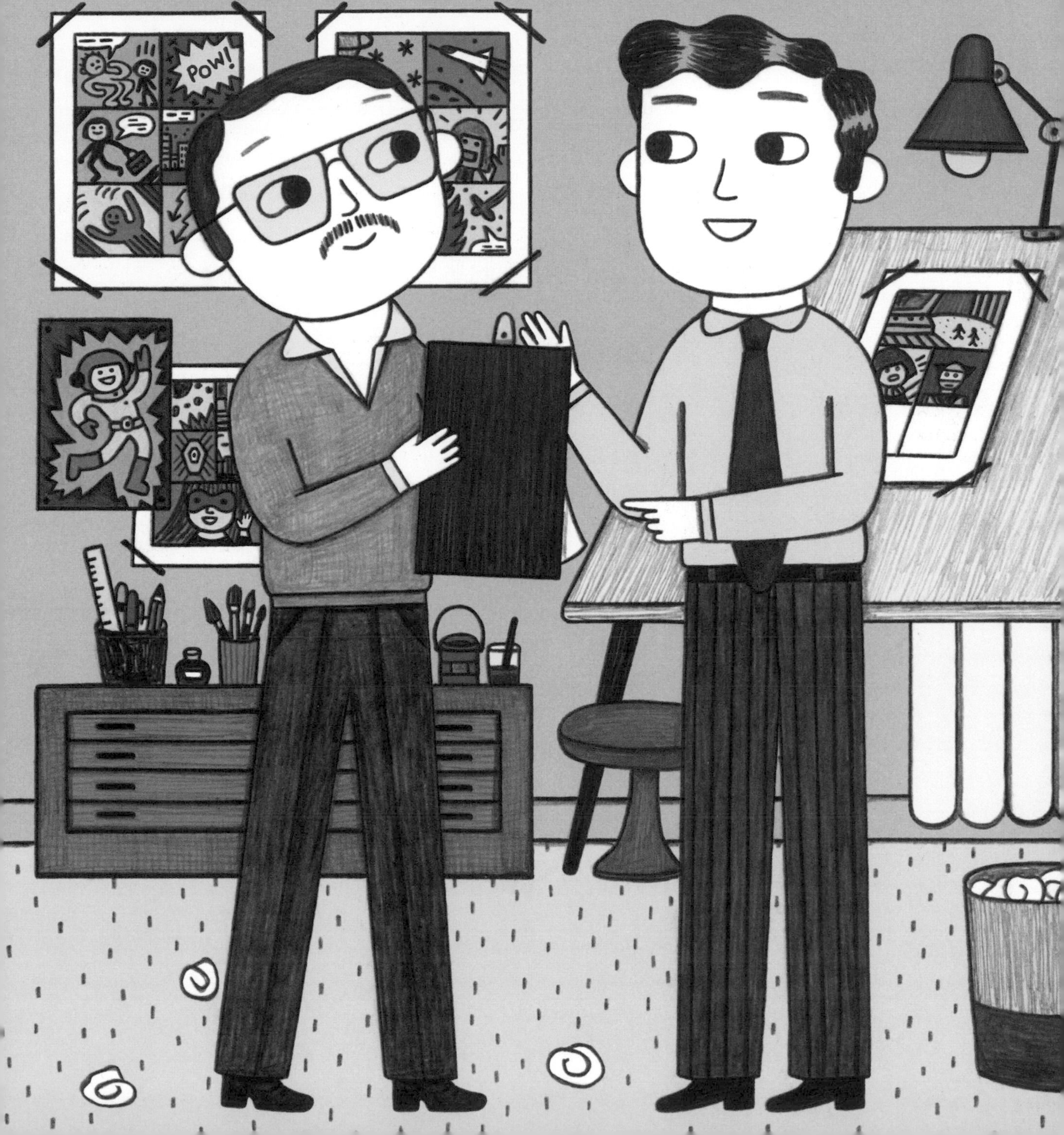
POW!

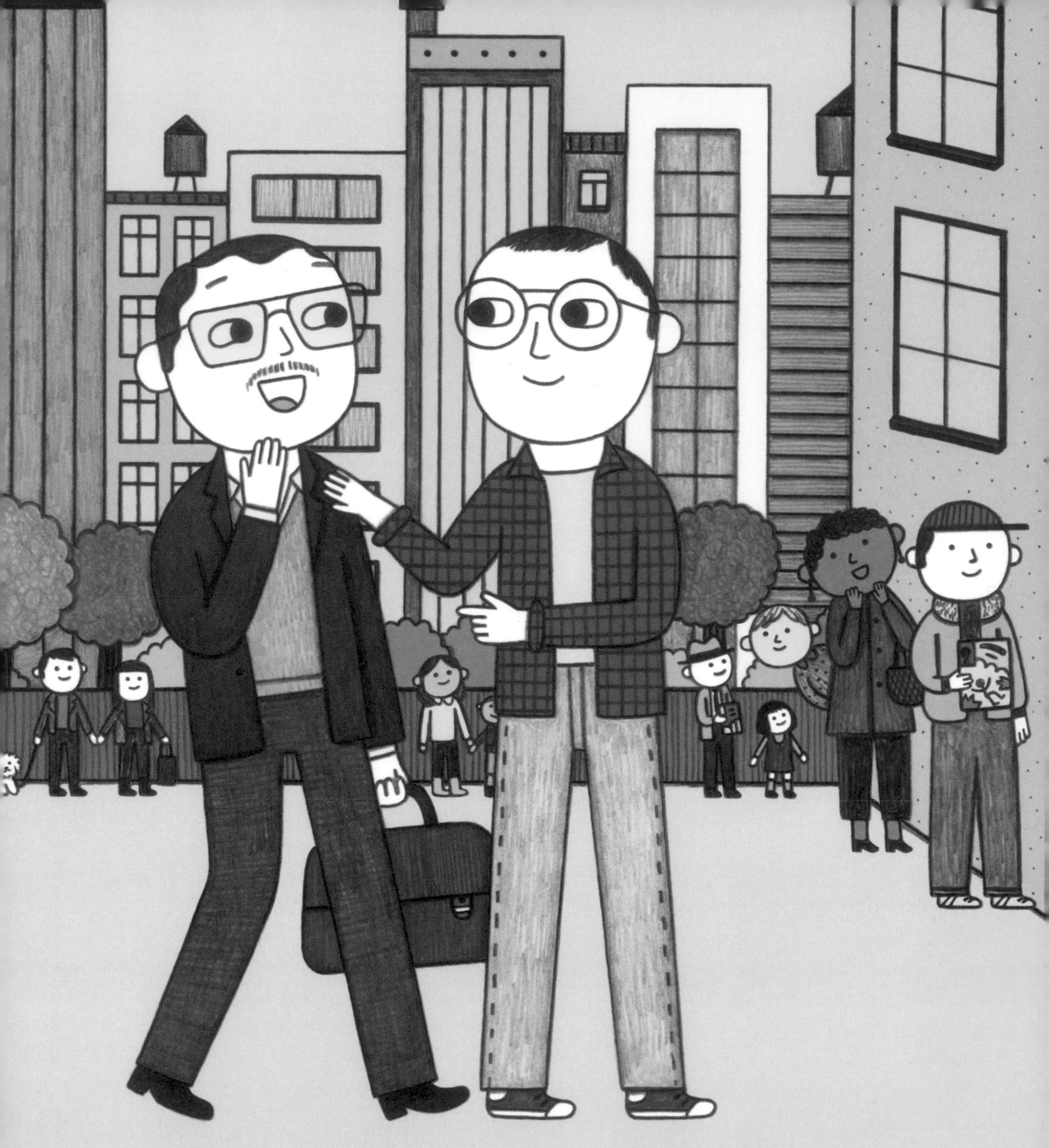

One year later, Stan and artist Steve Ditko created one of the company's most popular characters: Spider-Man.

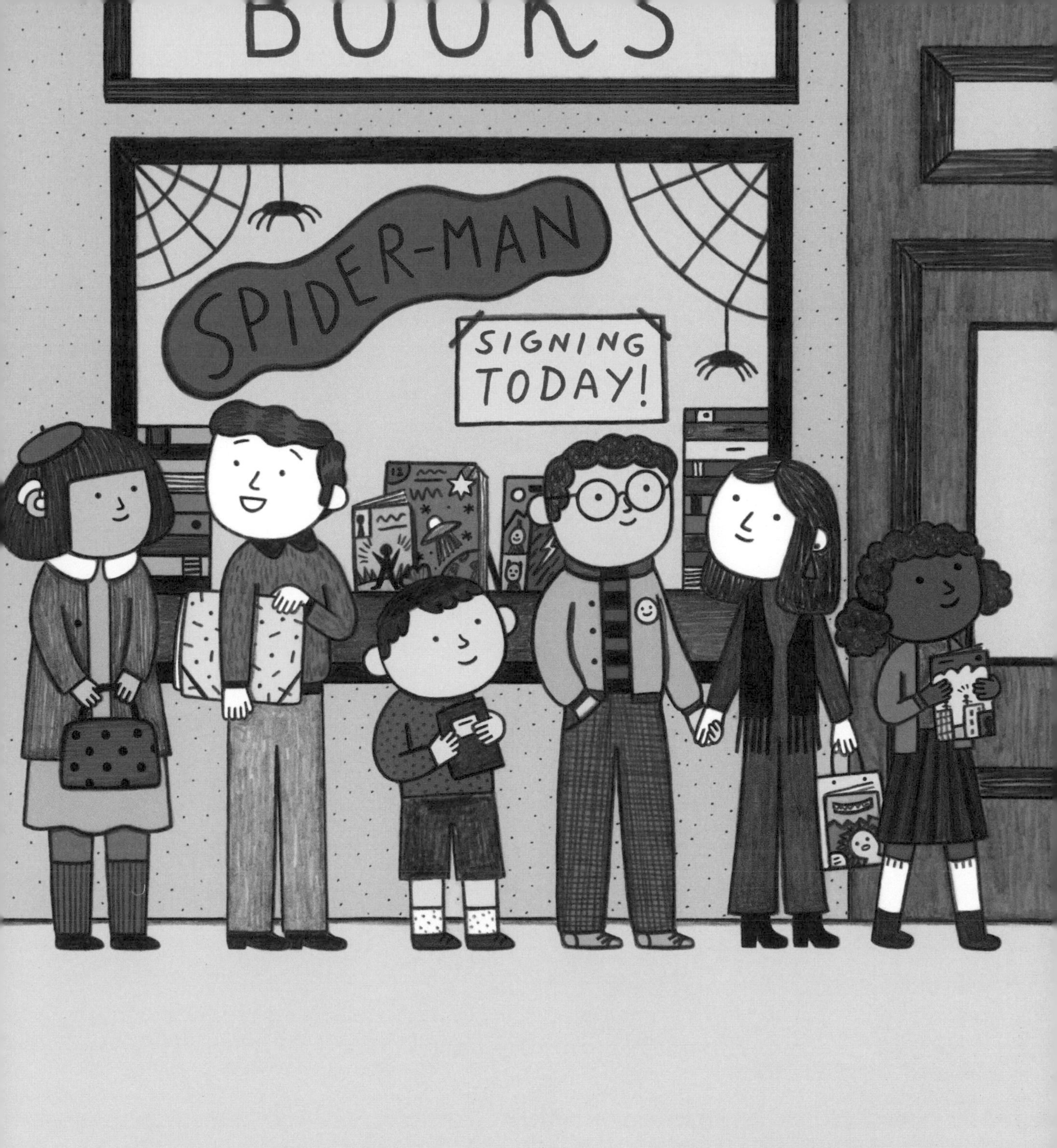
SPIDER-MAN
SIGNING TODAY!

The story was about Peter Parker, a regular teenager who faced the challenges of growing up while fighting crime as a superhero.

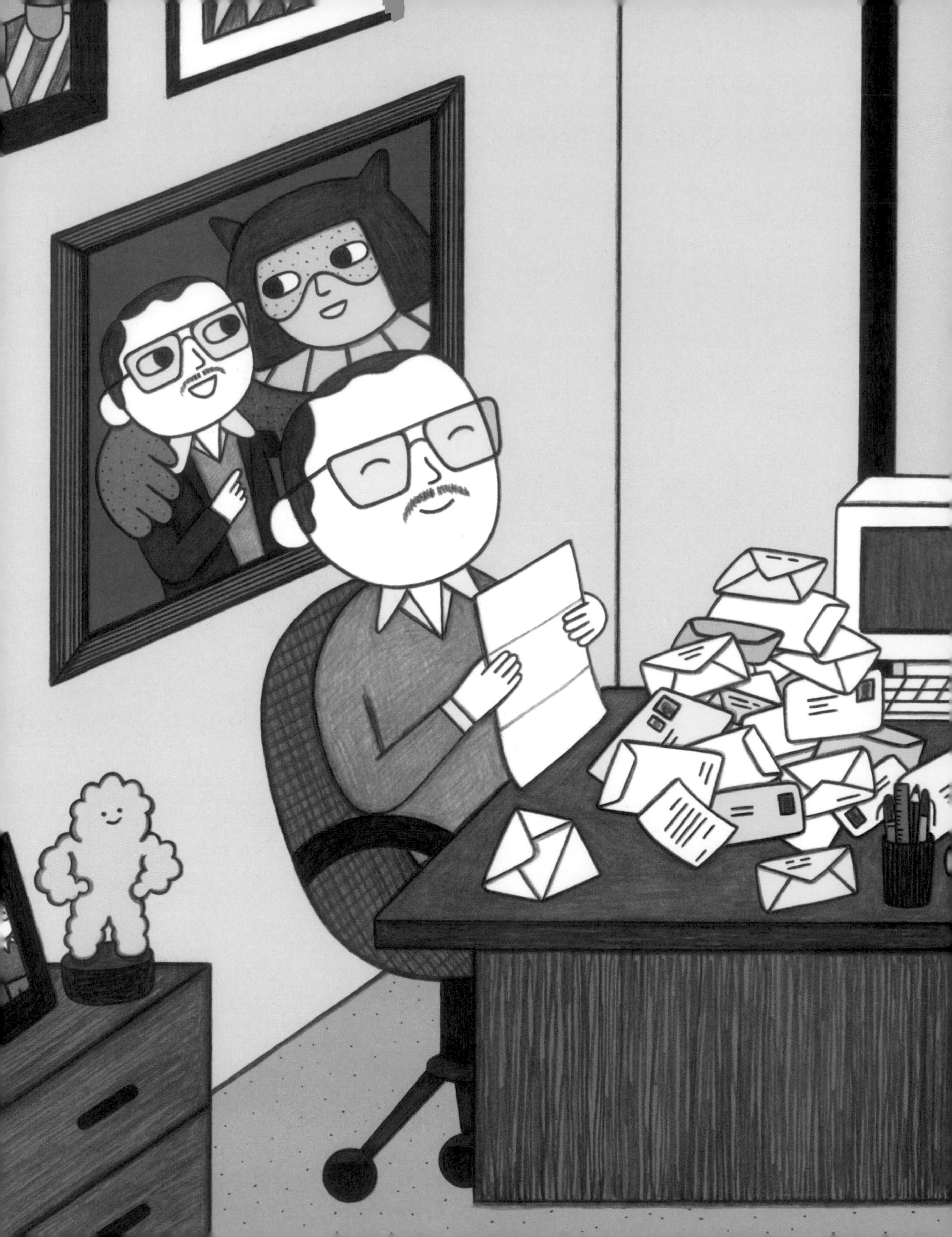

The Hulk, Thor, Iron Man, Doctor Strange, Falcon . . . Stan created a whole universe of superheroes. But he didn't stop there. He also built a bond between the comics' creators and fans, making them feel a part of a big community.

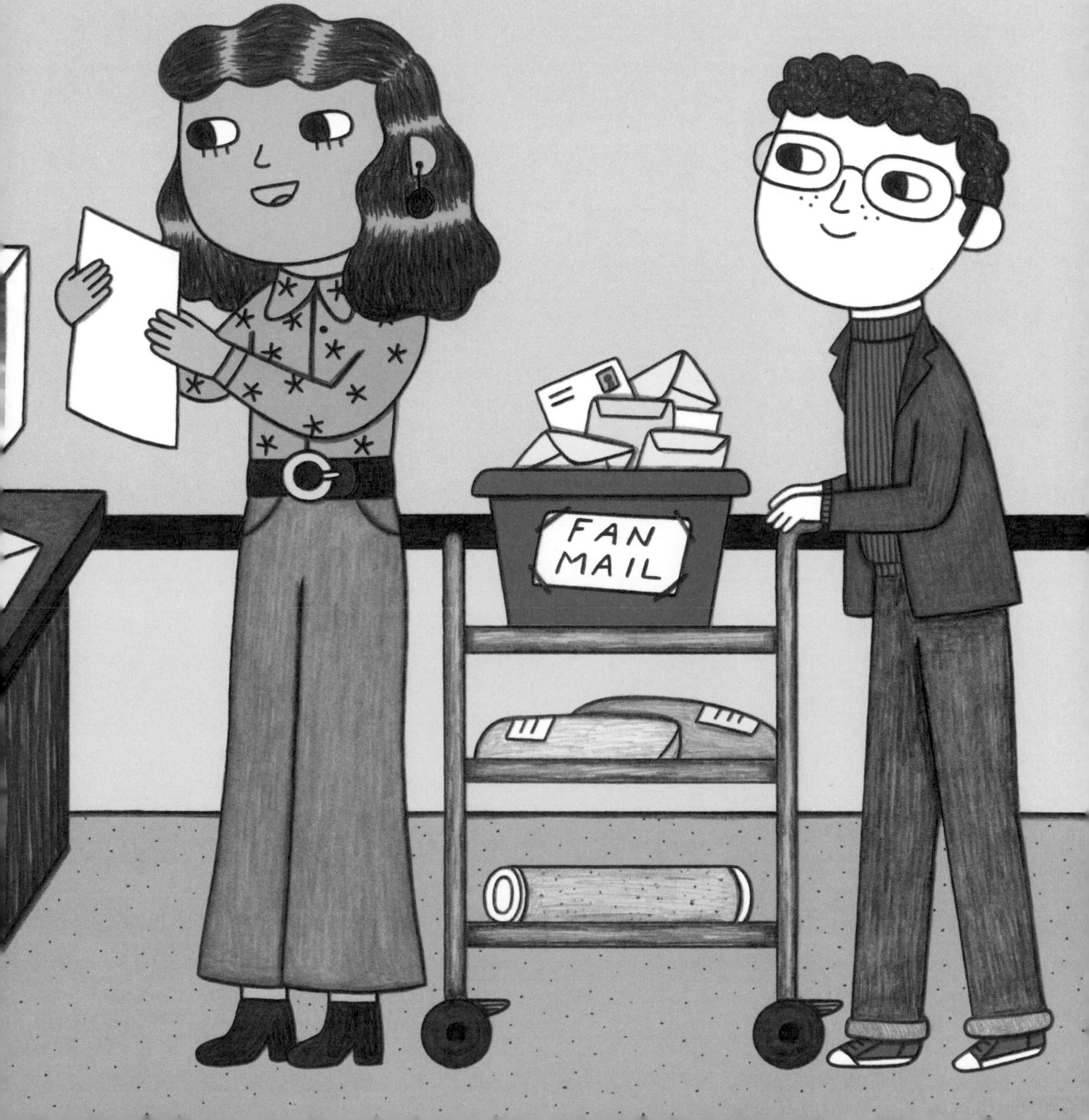
FAN MAIL

When his characters were taken to the screen, Stan didn't just sit back and watch. He loved to be involved and took on small acting roles in many of the films.

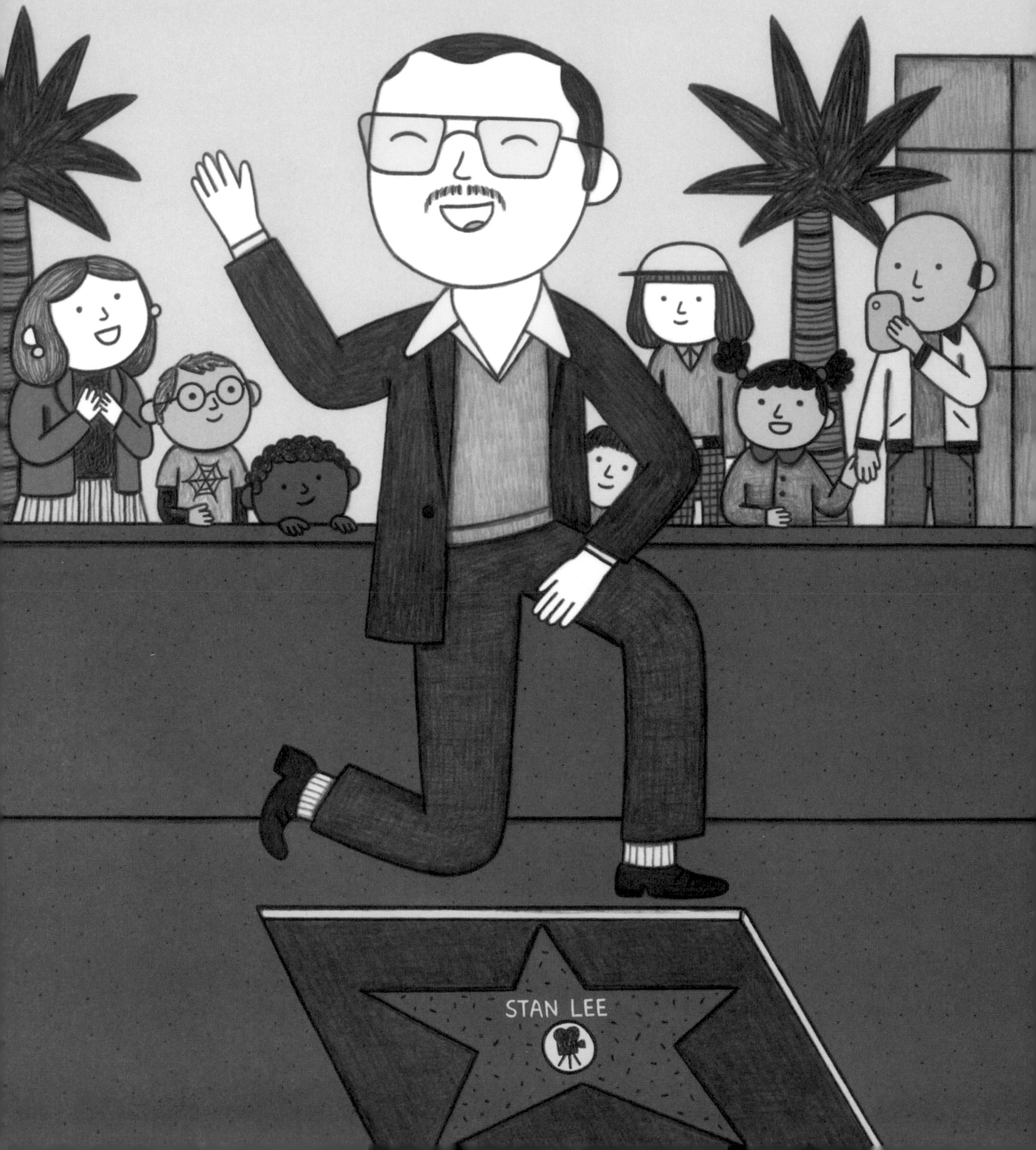
STAN LEE

Through his foundation, he also helped kids learn the skills he valued most: reading, writing, and drawing.

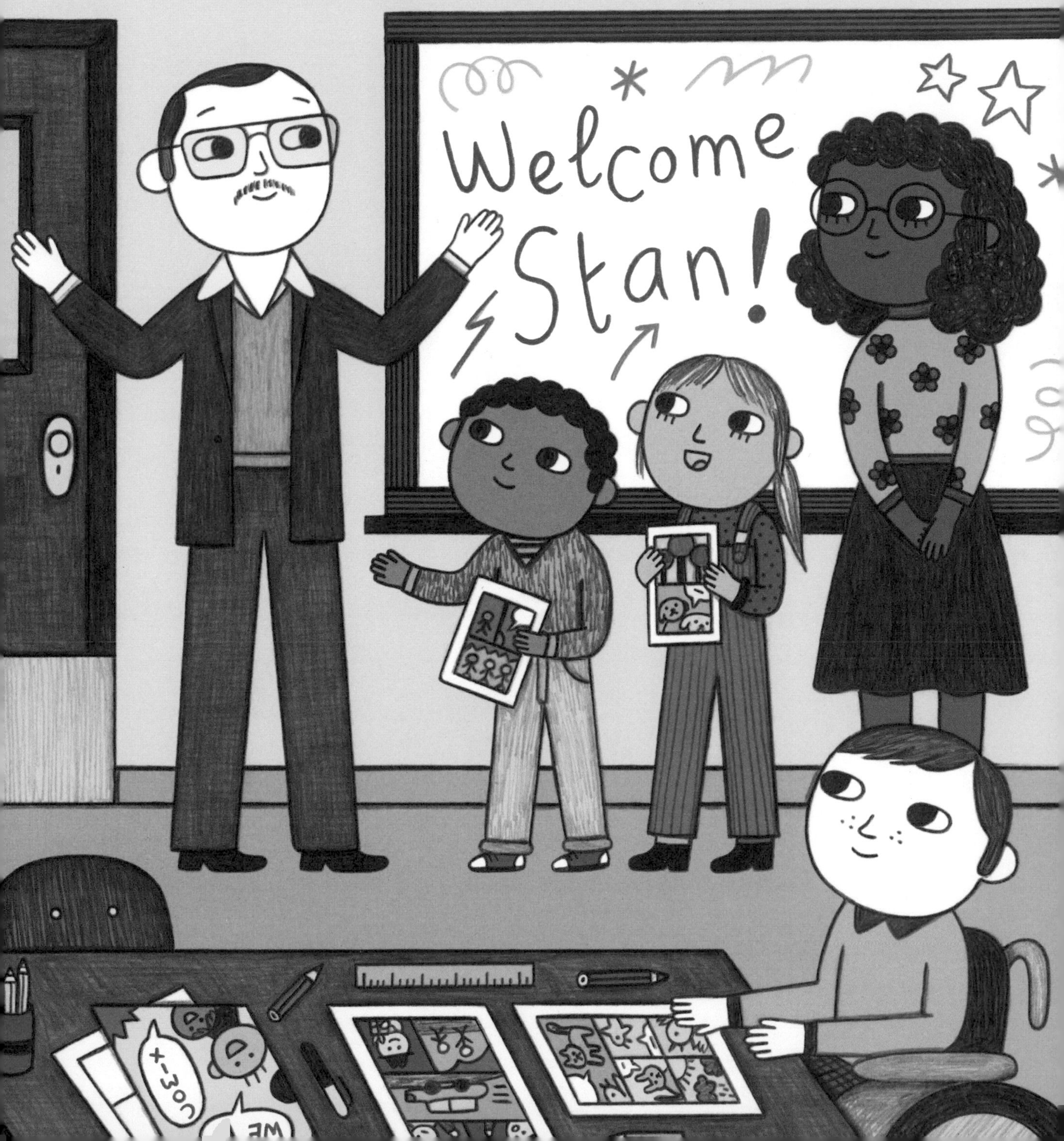
Welcome Stan!

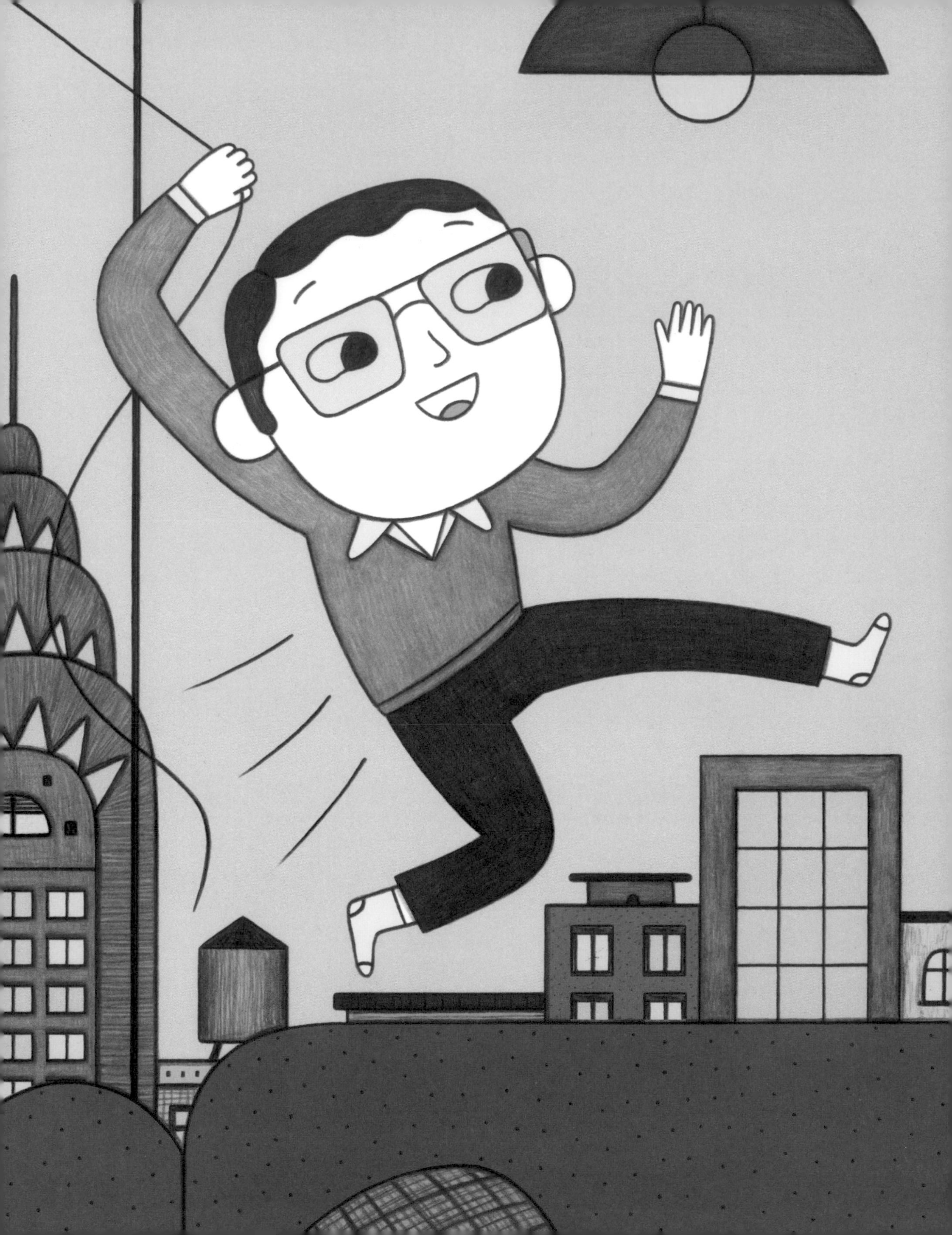

And that's how a regular kid named Stanley became the legendary Stan Lee, proving that you don't need superpowers to be a hero. It's the creativity, passion, and belief in ourselves that make us all extraordinary.

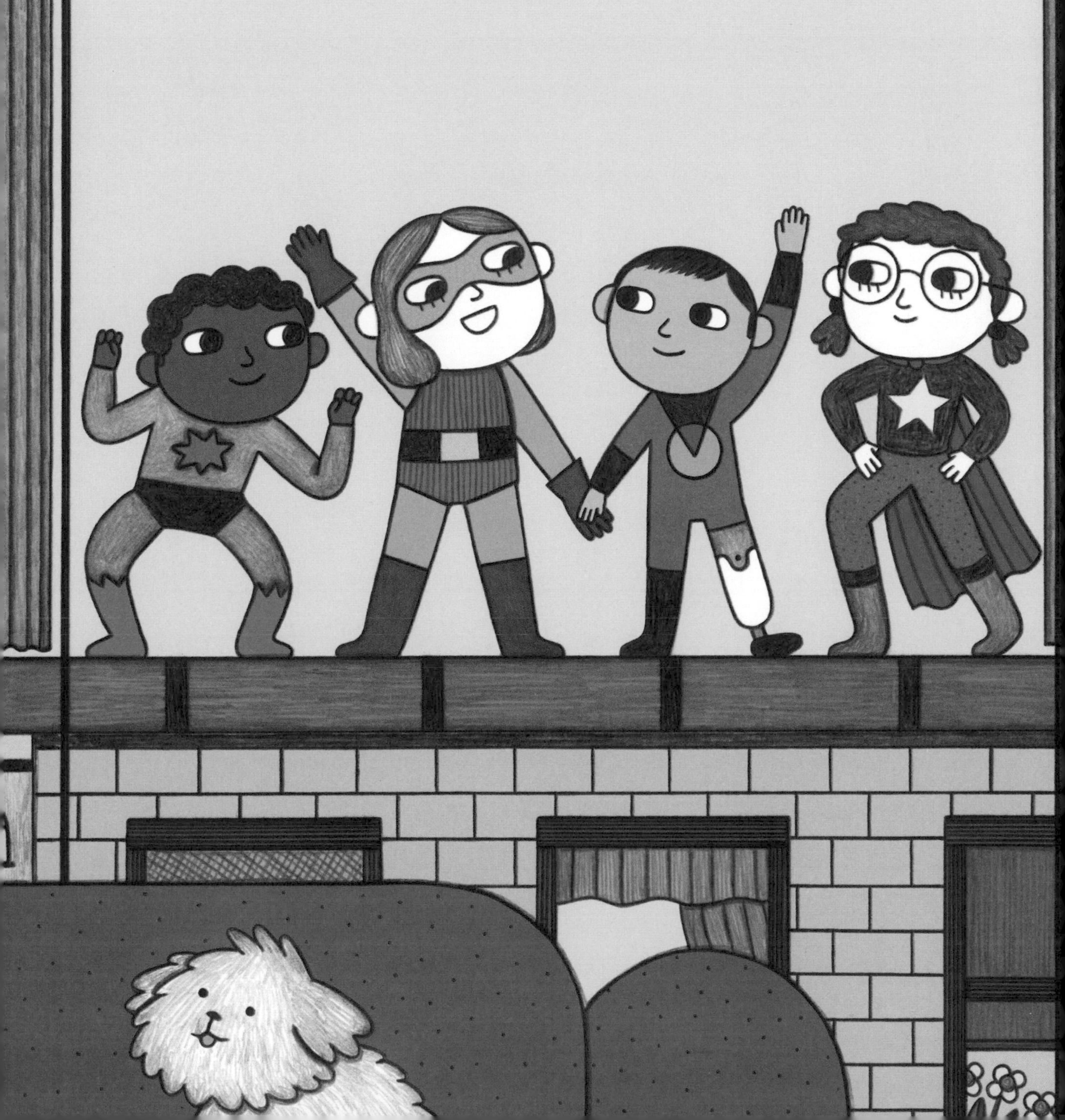

STAN LEE

(Born 1922 – Died 2018)

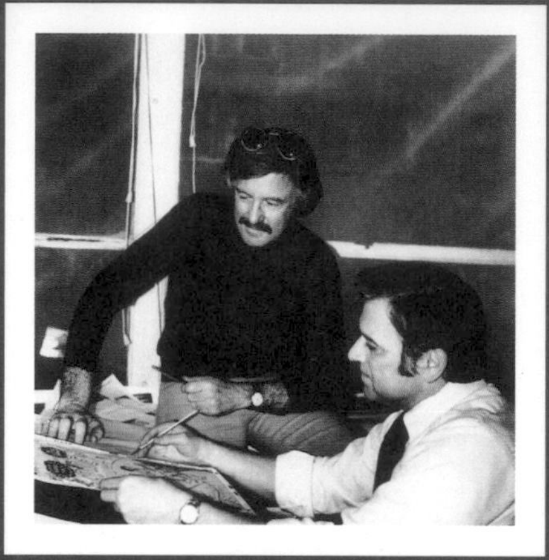

1975

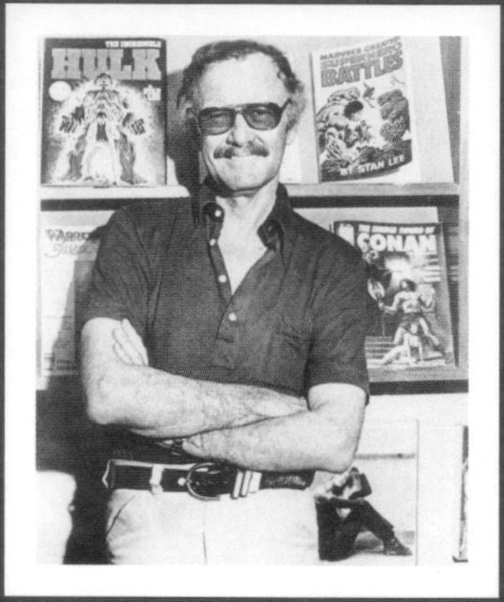
HULK
CONAN

1988

Stanley Martin Lieber grew up in New York City with his mom, dad, and brother, Larry. His parents were Jewish immigrants who moved to the U.S. from Romania. Stan's family didn't have much money, so he made his own fun. As a child, he would ride his bike around the city imagining he was a knight on horseback. In elementary school, he met an inspiring teacher named Mr. Ginsberg, who used humor and storytelling to keep the class interested. This made a big impression on Stan, and when he was older, he used a similar style in his writing. After high school, he joined Timely Comics as an assistant and was soon promoted to editor—a role he stayed in for thirty-one years. The company became Marvel and Stan helped create some of its best-loved characters, from Iron Man to

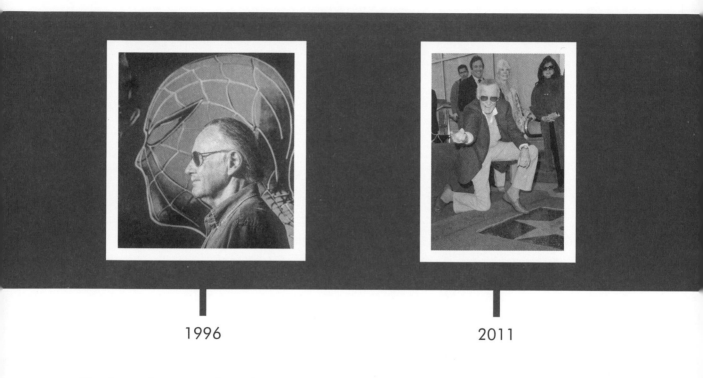

1996   2011

Black Panther. As editor, he started a column—a personal piece of writing—called "Stan's Soapbox." Here he shared his thoughts about the Marvel world and life outside and began to use his now famous sign-off "Excelsior!" In the 1980s, he moved to California to develop television shows about his characters. It was tough, but Stan worked hard and helped create several hits. When the Marvel Cinematic Universe boomed years later, he stayed involved by taking on small acting roles, called cameos, in numerous films. Until the end of his life, he loved connecting with fans and attended many comic conventions. Stan's story reminds us that we all have the power to make the world a better place. As he said to Peter Parker in *Spider-Man 3*: "I guess one person can make a difference."

Want to find out more about **Stan Lee**?

Have a read of these great books:

The Story of Stan Lee: A Biography Book for New Readers by Frank Berrios

With Great Power: The Marvelous Stan Lee by Annie Hunter Eriksen and Lee Gatlin

Original idea of the series by Maria Isabel Sánchez Vegara, published by Alba Editorial, s.l.u.
"Little People, BIG DREAMS" and "Pequeña & Grande" are trademarks of
Alba Editorial s.l.u. and/or Beautifool Couple S.L.
First Published in the USA in 2024 by Frances Lincoln Children's Books, an imprint of The Quarto Group.
100 Cummings Center, Suite 265D, Beverly, MA 01915, USA. T +1 978-282-9590 **www.Quarto.com**

A CIP record for this book is available from the Library of Congress.
ISBN 978-0-7112-9210-9
eBook ISBN 978-0-7112-9212-3
Set in Futura BT.

Published by Peter Marley · Designed by Sasha Moxon
Commissioned by Lucy Menzies · Edited by Molly Mead
Production by Nikki Ingram and Robin Boothroyd

Manufactured in Shanghai, China CC072024
3 5 7 9 8 6 4 2

Photographic acknowledgments (pages 28-29, from left to right): 1. Stan Lee, in dark sweater, publisher and editor of Marvel Comics, and his art director, John Romita, look at a drawing on March 5, 1975, which will appear in a comic book © Associated Press via Alamy Stock Photo. 2. COMIC BOOK CONFIDENTIAL, Stan Lee, 1988 © Cinecom/courtesy of Everett Collection Inc via Alamy Stock Photo. 3. LOS ANGELES, CA – JUNE 6: Comic book illustrator and creator Stan Lee in Los Angeles, California on June 6, 1996 © Evan Hurd via Alamy Stock Photo. 4. Stan Lee honored with a Star on the Hollywood Walk of Fame in Los Angeles, 2011 © Tsuni / USA via Alamy Stock Photo.

MIX
Paper | Supporting responsible forestry
FSC® C008047
FSC www.fsc.org

Collect the *Little People*, **BIG DREAMS**™ series:

| FRIDA KAHLO | COCO CHANEL | MAYA ANGELOU | AMELIA EARHART | AGATHA CHRISTIE | MARIE CURIE | ROSA PARKS | AUDREY HEPBURN | EMMELINE PANKHURST |

FRIDA KAHLO • COCO CHANEL • MAYA ANGELOU • AMELIA EARHART • AGATHA CHRISTIE • MARIE CURIE • ROSA PARKS • AUDREY HEPBURN • EMMELINE PANKHURST

ELLA FITZGERALD • ADA LOVELACE • JANE AUSTEN • GEORGIA O'KEEFFE • HARRIET TUBMAN • ANNE FRANK • MOTHER TERESA • JOSEPHINE BAKER • L. M. MONTGOMERY

JANE GOODALL • SIMONE DE BEAUVOIR • MUHAMMAD ALI • STEPHEN HAWKING • MARIA MONTESSORI • VIVIENNE WESTWOOD • MAHATMA GANDHI • DAVID BOWIE • WILMA RUDOLPH

DOLLY PARTON • BRUCE LEE • RUDOLF NUREYEV • ZAHA HADID • MARY SHELLEY • MARTIN LUTHER KING JR. • DAVID ATTENBOROUGH • ASTRID LINDGREN • EVONNE GOOLAGONG

BOB DYLAN • ALAN TURING • BILLIE JEAN KING • GRETA THUNBERG • JESSE OWENS • JEAN-MICHEL BASQUIAT • ARETHA FRANKLIN • CORAZON AQUINO • PELÉ

ERNEST SHACKLETON • STEVE JOBS • AYRTON SENNA • LOUISE BOURGEOIS • ELTON JOHN • JOHN LENNON • PRINCE • CHARLES DARWIN • CAPTAIN TOM MOORE

HANS CHRISTIAN ANDERSEN • STEVIE WONDER • MEGAN RAPINOE • MARY ANNING • MALALA YOUSAFZAI • ANDY WARHOL • RUPAUL • MICHELLE OBAMA • MINDY KALING

IRIS APFEL | ROSALIND FRANKLIN | RUTH BADER GINSBURG | MARILYN MONROE | KAMALA HARRIS | ALBERT EINSTEIN | CHARLES DICKENS | YOKO ONO | MICHAEL JORDAN

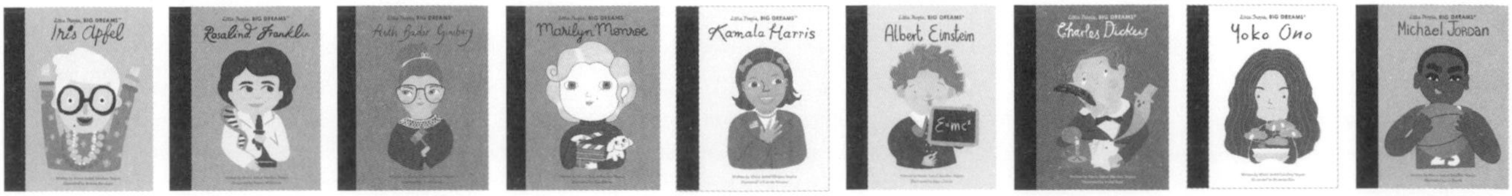

NELSON MANDELA | PABLO PICASSO | AMANDA GORMAN | GLORIA STEINEM | FLORENCE NIGHTINGALE | HARRY HOUDINI | J.R.R. TOLKIEN | ELVIS PRESLEY | NEIL ARMSTRONG

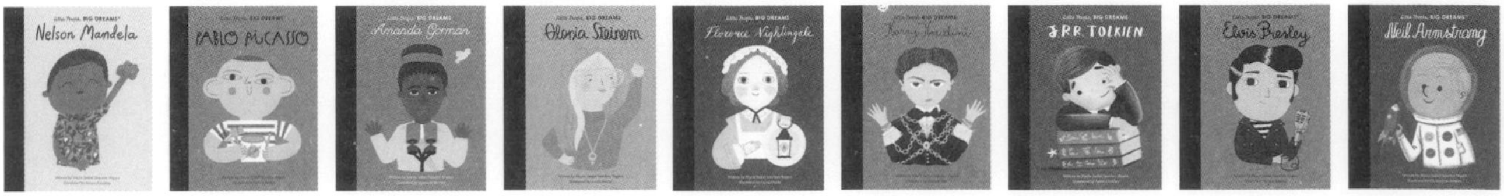

ALEXANDER VON HUMBOLDT | NIKOLA TESLA | WILMA MANKILLER | MARCUS RASHFORD | LAVERNE COX | MAE JEMISON | DWAYNE JOHNSON | HELEN KELLER | ANNA PAVLOVA

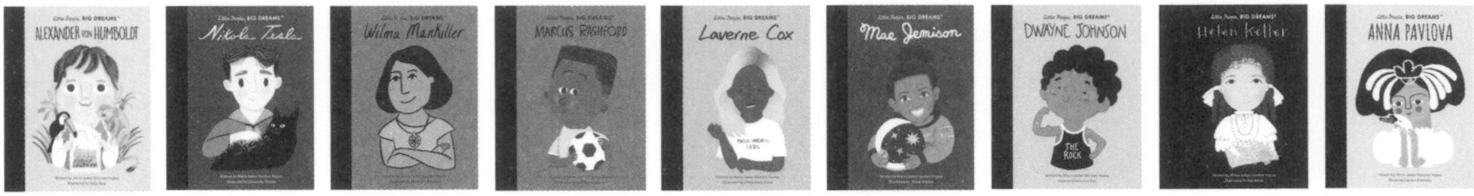

QUEEN ELIZABETH | TERRY FOX | HEDY LAMARR | SHAKIRA | FREDDIE MERCURY | LEWIS HAMILTON | LOUIS PASTEUR | PRINCESS DIANA | DAVID HOCKNEY

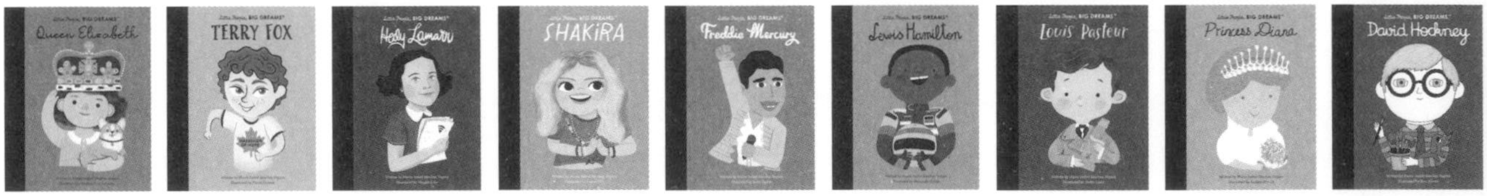

VANESSA NAKATE | OLIVE MORRIS | KING CHARLES | MOZART | STEVE IRWIN | JÜRGEN KLOPP | LEO MESSI | SALLY RIDE | TENZING NORGAY

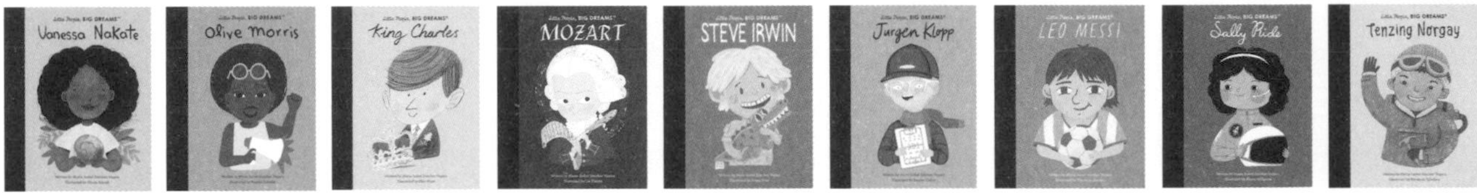

KYLIE MINOGUE | BEYONCÉ | TAYLOR SWIFT | RAFA NADAL | USAIN BOLT | SIMONE BILES

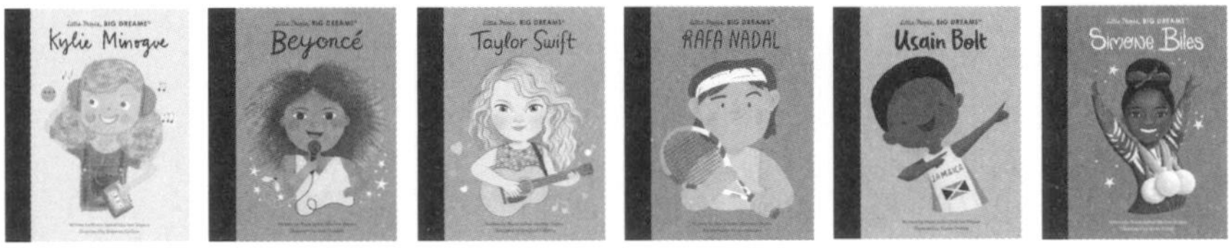

STAN LEE | LEONARD COHEN | DAVID BECKHAM | VINCENT VAN GOGH | MARY KOM

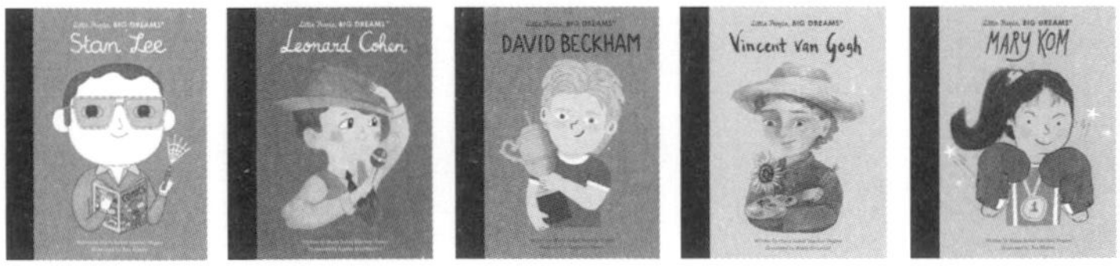

Scan the QR code for free activity sheets, teachers' notes and more information about the series at www.littlepeoplebigdreams.com

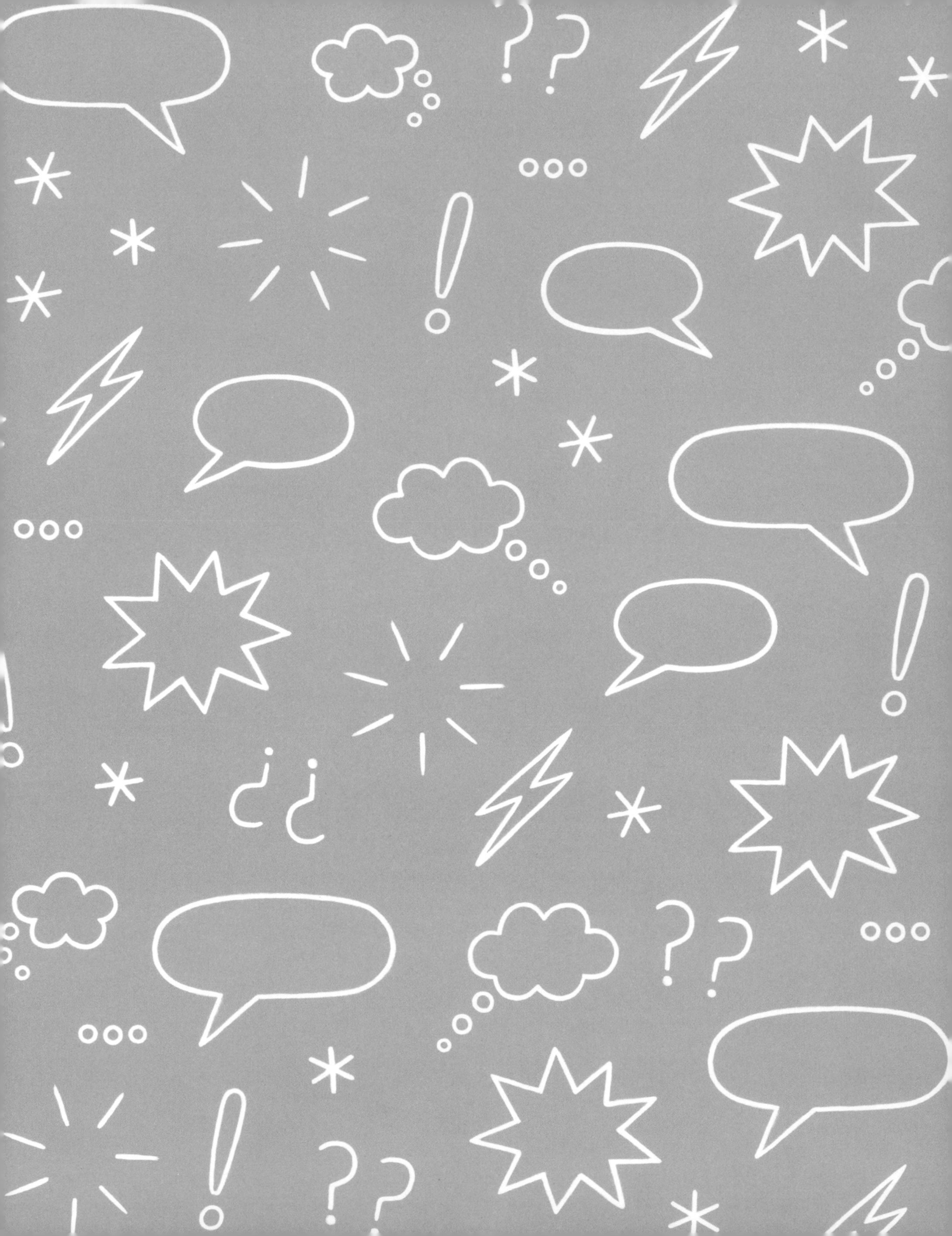